MEDICAL LEAVE

Adam Weiss

Medical Leave is a work of fiction. Names, characters, places, and incidents are products of the author's imagination or are used fictitiously. Any resemblance to actual persons, living or dead, businesses, companies, events, or locales is entirely coincidental.

Printed in the United States of America.

First Edition

ISBN: 979-8-9932884-0-6

Library of Congress Cataloging-in-Publication Data has been applied for.

Book design by Adam Weiss

For my mom, and children, Rachel and Brandon,
and for my partner in life, Nancy — love you all.

"By our own faculty of intelligence and understanding, we can distinguish between good and evil, doing as we choose. Nothing holds us back from making this choice between good and evil—the power is in our hands."

— Maimonides, twelfth century.

PROLOGUE

The unseasonably hot weather front enveloped Linosa in a stifling blanket of humidity. The tiny island, a mere 260 kilometers from Tunisia, nestled in the Mediterranean Sea, had become an unexpected hub of activity. By six a.m., the eastern village, once a sleepy backwater, now buzzed with the relentless clamor of construction. It seemed to only take days; those three new blocks materialized, their sleek facades a stark contrast to the island's rustic charm. Locals whispered about the rapid pace of development, attributing a good deal of it to foreign workers. Yet, the newly erected buildings—designed by celebrity architects—seemed to loom over the island with an unsettling presence.

These modern monoliths, dubbed "Beverly Hills" by the islanders, were more than just symbols of wealth. They were fortresses—guarded by armed sentinels, windows shrouded in darkness, and courtyards adorned with flourishing flowers that concealed a darker reality. Beneath the veneer of luxury, a clandestine world thrived. The wealthy elite, shielded from prying eyes, conducted their affairs in opulence and secrecy. Free Wi-Fi and satellite TV in multiple languages were the least of the island's offerings. What truly drew the attention of powerful figures was absolute discretion.

The island had become a playground for shadowy offshore accounts and the notorious individuals who controlled them. Hidden within the gated community were criminals of every stripe—South American cartel bosses, terrorists under the scrutiny of the United Nations, and a motley crew of former world leaders and bankers. Together, they represented the most untouchable, dangerous elements of society. Beneath the surface, their fortunes and influence were entangled in a web of hidden transactions.

Among the throngs of expatriates and well-heeled residents enjoying the island's luxuries exist a pristine ivory tower that stood out even among the lavish structures. At 4A Beverly Hill Street, a state-of-the-art medical clinic and spa catering to its elite clientele for over a decade. The likes of Middle Eastern dignitaries and European celebrities frequented its sterile halls for discreet procedures. Cosmetic surgery, heart treatments—nothing viable too big or small for the European surgeons who worked there, operating in silence, lured by hefty sums and ironclad confidentiality agreements.

But on this particular day, the quiet order of the clinic was about to be shattered.

Inside one of the clinic's operating rooms, the air was thick with tension. The patient, a notorious ex-Syrian banker, lay sedated on the table. His presence on the island was no mere coincidence. Entangled in a web of arms trafficking and human smuggling and terrorist cells like group 786, he had evaded international capture. The United Nations sought his capture as well as Interpol, and the United States—but here, on Linosa, he was untouchable. His influence a shield, and armed guards— hulking men with Glocks visible beneath their ill-fitting jackets— were his sword. They sat in the waiting room, oblivious to the unfolding chaos.

What should have been a routine hip replacement became a spiraling disaster. The Italian surgeon scheduled for the operation vanished, incapacitated by a night of excessive drinking. Desperate, Valeria Perez, the clinic's director, made a frantic call to Doctor Solutions—a last-resort organization known for dispatching physicians to the world's most dangerous and desperate corners.

Valeria is a formidable woman. At thirty-five, with her perfectly groomed hair with a light milk chocolate complexion and meticulous appearance on her five-foot seven tone frame, she commanded respect. Her keen intellect and unwavering professionalism propelled her to the top of her field, but today, even she felt the pressure. She knew the stakes. The patient on the table was no ordinary man. A delay may trigger catastrophic consequences. With no further options, she reluctantly accepted Doctor Solutions' offer: an American surgeon, already on the island. However, a complication arose. The director's nerves were on edge as she paced the clinic, awaiting the arrival of this mystery doctor.

Thirty minutes later, she greeted the doctor at a side entrance, the patient's chart in hand. The American being tall, broad-shouldered, with an air of casual confidence. His brown wavy hair and striking green eyes gave him a roguish charm, hard to ignore.

"We have a seventy-eight-year-old hypertensive, obese male with multiple stents, a history of blood thinners, and recreational drug use. He requires a hip replacement," she said briskly.

"Good morning to you, too," he replied, his voice deep and smooth, with just a hint of amusement. He took the chart from her hand. "I've done this procedure more times than I can count. You don't need to worry."

Valeria's mind raced. Something about the doctor's easy confidence unsettled her. He had a magnetic presence and disarming charm, but she couldn't afford distractions. "One more thing," her tone sharp. "Keep your face covered with a mask at all times, and don't speak any English. Better yet, don't speak at all."

"No problem," the doctor said with a smirk. "I can play the mystery man."

With that, she spun around on her Louboutin Stelios and darted off to more problems needing solutions.

In the operating room, a nurse helped the American surgeon with the surgical gloves after disinfecting his hands. The anesthesia nurse placed the patient under deeper sedation, and within minutes, the banker began snoring with a tracheal tube inserted. Telltale signs of heart congestion thought the American as he stepped forward to the operating table. Doing the procedure with the patient on their side, going from posterior, involved cutting muscles to get to the hip. Due to his obesity, the patient lay supine.

Under normal situations, the surgical team would perform the frontal operation using a less-invasive technique.

The surgeon found this suitable because the femoral triangle, a concept familiar to every first-year student in the dissection lab, started by showcasing the wonders of the functionality of the human body to the students. Some of the most vital vascular components and nerves ran through the region adjacent to the groin.

The doctor worked with swift precision. The team, unaware of the full scope of the situation, followed his lead. But as he made the incision, a strange calm fell over him. His hands moved with deadly intent, cutting through muscle and fat as if on autopilot. This was no ordinary surgery. The doctor had a mission—a mission to ensure that this patient never left the table alive.

He worked his scalpel around the pelvic bone at a 45-degree angle to the hip joint. A simple guess because the size of the patient's thigh and stomach distorted the anatomy. He took a separator and yanked the thigh region open, revealing layers of yellow adipose tissue and little else. While removing the excess tissue and swiftly filled the bio-hazard bucket at his feet. The doctor glanced at the patient's face, noting the bloated jowls and deep creases around the closed eyes. He pondered if the patient may perhaps recognize him after all these years? The American pointed across the room at the larger container, and the nurse turned to get it.

Then chaos erupted. Alarms blared as the patient's vitals plummeted. The surgical team scrambled, but the doctor remained eerily calm. Blood gushed from the incision, coating the room in a crimson spray. The surgical nurse, in her panic, slipped and crashed to the floor, her head hitting the metal table with a sickening thud.

With each heartbeat, the patient's life was draining away as he neared death. The staff's frantic attempts to stabilize him proved futile. The doctor already sealed his fate. He intentionally sliced through the femoral artery, yanking it out and causing the dramatic gusher in the room. He placed the clamps on the layers of fat to make it appear as if he tried to clamp off the artery. While asking for the extra waste bin, distracting the nurse, he removed a syringe filled with blood thinner and jammed it into the femoral vein for good measure before dropping it into the bio-hazard bucket.

In the aftermath, the American slipped out of the operating room, leaving behind a trail of destruction. He washed his hands methodically, ridding them of any evidence. The mission completed and an enemy of justice died and retribution for the children of the Lebanese camp that felt like a lifetime ago.

As he boarded a sleek Riva Tritone, bound for the succeeding phase of his mission, the doctor reflected on the path ahead. The waters of the Mediterranean stretched before him, dark and dangerous. It had become more than just a game of cat and mouse. It was a war—a war fought in the shadows, where the lines between hero and villain blurred, certainty only existed in death.

CHAPTER 1

Flechtheim Gallery, Bern, Switzerland

The streets of Bern were deserted, bathed in the soft glow of street lamps. Flechtheim Gallery, renowned across Europe for its impeccable art collection, was locking its doors for the evening. DovBer Flechtheim, the gallery's elderly proprietor, moved with the slow grace of someone accustomed to routine. His tailored overcoat scarcely shielded him from the biting cold, and he muttered to himself, annoyed at having forgotten his hat—again. Bern's night air, crisp and unforgiving, seemed intent on reminding him of his age. As he pulled his coat tighter around him, he reflected on his family's legacy.

The Flechtheims always valued tradition. For over a century, the gallery remained in their hands, passed down from generation to generation. DovBer took pride in closing the shop himself each night, despite his children's protests. They insisted he delegate the responsibility. "Times are changing, father," they would say, their voices filled with concern. "You don't need to do this anymore." Yet, DovBer clung to the ritual. In a world that had grown unrecognizable to him, this was the one thing that hadn't changed.

The Flechtheim family grew wealthy, yet their fortune hadn't dampened their philanthropic spirit. They donated numerous priceless works of art to prestigious museums around the world, refusing to sell even when presented with staggering offers. Recently, a surge of interest from Asian buyers reignited international attention on their collection. DovBer found himself fielding offers that dwarfed those made by Japanese collectors in the 1980s. His children urged him to retire, to consider selling. But DovBer, now in his late seventies, had no interest in leaving the gallery behind. "Retire to what?" he would say. "My love is gone, and all I have left is a dog to remind me of her." He thought of Woman in Red, the Peter Klee painting that hung in secret behind a false wall in his bedroom above the fireplace. Never used, and one needed to bend and reach into and turn their hand backwards to press the release button.

His wife used to tell him that someday, he may well get his arm stuck in there. He couldn't bear to give up that one item, the last connection to his late wife.

Yet, rumors circulated—rumors of art thefts targeting private collectors. His children's anxiety increased. Against DovBer's protests, they hired a bodyguard. Eitan, an ex-Israeli soldier, handsome with an intimidating presence, assigned to protect both the gallery and DovBer. Eitan's skills in Krav Maga were well-known, and though Bern prohibited weapons, Eitan's sheer physicality was enough to reassure DovBer's family. Over time, the elderly man grew to appreciate Eitan, sharing stories of the gallery's rich history. DovBer even indulged Eitan in conversations about the finer points of art—a subject that, to his surprise, the soldier took a genuine interest in.

Julie Kellenberg, the gallery's young assistant, another source of solace. Her professionalism is only matched by her grace. She had a warmth about her that didn't go unnoticed by

Eitan. After months of subtle smiles and lingering glances, Eitan finally mustered the courage to ask her out. The two struck up a romance, their connection providing Eitan with a reprieve from his duties. After her work hours she would leave earlier and go to Flechtheim's flat, which was her routine. The family paid her extra to see that their father had a meal delivered at 6 pm. She would wait for the delivery and place it on the smaller kitchen table facing the window towards the interior courtyard of his flat.

He put up a fuss about the poor girl working more hours than needed, but after a month, he looked forward to the meals. Julie pulled out all the stops, ensuring that a variety of food would be delivered.

As DovBer rounded the corner to his flat, the wind picked up, biting at his exposed skin. His hands trembled as he fumbled with the keys, his arthritic fingers betraying him. Suddenly, a voice pierced the quiet.

"Let me help you with that."

DovBer flinched. He hadn't heard anyone approach. The stranger loomed over him; his face obscured by a hood. His presence was unsettling, too close for comfort. Fear gripped DovBer's chest, but it quickly eased when he saw the brown delivery bag the man held. The tension melted away.

"Oh, thank you," DovBer replied, offering his keys. "It's labeled 'Flat five.'"

The man took the keys with a nod, his gloved hands moving deftly. DovBer couldn't place the accent—foreign, but not Swiss. He wore gloves, which struck DovBer as odd, given the temperature didn't warrant such attire for a Swiss. A ripple of unease crawled up his spine, but he dismissed it. He was tired. Surely, this is just another delivery.

"Is that for Flat D-Five?" DovBer asked, trying to sound casual.

"Yes, it is," the hooded man replied curtly.

DovBer adjusted his glasses, squinting at the man's face. Something wasn't right. His instincts, honed from years of dealing with clients from every walk of life, screamed at him to leave. But the cold and fatigue clouded his judgment.

"Well, either my watch is off, or one of us is late," DovBer muttered. "I don't think I've ever had a delivery after I've returned home."

"Sorry, I'm new. Got kind of lost. It won't happen again," the man professed, offering a faint smile that never reached his eyes.

"That's alright. I get lost more frequently than I'd like to admit these days," DovBer chuckled, trying to mask his growing discomfort. "Here, let me take that from you, and be on your way."

"No, sir," the man said, his tone firm. "Full service. I'm to deliver to the flat, or I'll lose my job."

Something shifted in the man's demeanor. It was subtle, but DovBer noticed the glint of control in his eyes. As they stepped into the elevator, DovBer's unease deepened. The man pressed the button for the fifth floor, his gloved fingers moving with deliberate precision. The elevator doors slid shut with a hushed thud, and in that moment, DovBer knew—this wasn't good. His pulse quickened, and though he tried to convince himself otherwise, a deep, primal fear settled in his chest.

The rising elevator brought with it a growing internal chill. It gnawed at his bones, a warning he could no longer ignore. Trapped, he found himself in a situation he hadn't been in for years. DovBer Flechtheim felt truly vulnerable.

CHAPTER 2

The Heist

The elevator doors opened with a faint ding, revealing a dimly lit hallway. Neither DovBer nor the hooded man move right away. The silence stretched between them, tense and thick, broken except for a quiet hum of the elevator's mechanics.

DovBer's eyes flickered to the alarm button. Might it even work in this aging building? He hesitated, hand trembling as he reached for it.

The hooded man acted swiftly, seizing DovBer by his coat collar and dragging him out into the hallway. Weak and unsteady, the man was pushed forward, almost falling, like a child. His heart raced when he saw it—his flat door ajar.

Panic gripped him. His body trembled as the man nudged him through the open door. Inside, the scene that awaited him all but sent him into shock. A pair of legs—elegant, lifeless—stretched from the bedroom into the living room.

"What is going on? What do you want?" DovBer's voice cracked, his body trembling uncontrollably.

The hooded man remained silent, but a second figure emerged from the bedroom. Well-dressed, with a cool, calculating gaze, he walked over the body. His long knife, glistening in the dim light, wiped clean with one of DovBer's hand towels.

"Hello, Mr. Flechtheim," the man said, his English precise, chilling in its formality.

DovBer's eyes darted to the body. The blood-soaked blouse, the familiar blue skirt—Julie. His assistant. His friend. Lying dead in his flat.

"You monster!" DovBer's voice cracked. "Why? What did she ever do to you?"

"She was a Jew," the well-dressed man commented as if that explained everything. He sighed, almost bored with the situation. "Not my finest work, I'll admit. But what's done is done."

DovBer's anger boiled over. He lunged at the man, his fists raised, but his frail body was no match for the younger, stronger man. The assailant merely stepped back, his knife still in hand, watching the old man with a cold detachment.

"Enough theatrics, Mr. Flechtheim. We're here for the Peter Klee. We've had our eyes on it for some time."

The man pointed lazily at the ceiling. "We did some work next door. Placed a few cameras. There." He gestured towards the light fixture. "And there." He motioned to the bedroom door.

DovBer's breath caught in his throat. They knew. They been informed about Woman in Red.

"No," he muttered, shaking his head in disbelief. "No cameras. I'm on the building board. We don't allow modifications…"

But the man wasn't listening. He moved closer, his knife now glinting in the light.

Flechtheim's mind raced, trying to comprehend the

situation. The Woman in Red. They came for it. His carefulness and secrecy were remarkable. How did they know?

"We placed cameras here weeks ago, while you went on your weekend trip to Paris." the man explained, sensing DovBer's confusion. "Disguised them during the 'renovations' next door. We had access to the partnering wall, and all was approved by the building's board members in your absence. We've been watching you, Mr. Flechtheim."

Flechtheim's face paled. The cameras. The renovations. It had all been a ruse. For weeks, or even longer, they'd been plotting this.

"I don't know what you're talking about," Flechtheim stammered, though his voice lacked conviction. "There's no Peter Klee here."

The knife-wielder sighed, a flicker of impatience crossing his face. "We can do this the easy way, or the hard way. But we will find it."

Before Flechtheim could respond, the door burst open with a thunderous crash. Eitan stormed into the flat, his eyes locking onto the hooded thug. Without hesitation, he charged, his training kicking in as he engaged the larger man in a vicious struggle.

The flat erupted into chaos. Eitan grappled with the hooded man, their bodies colliding with furniture, sending chairs and tables crashing. But the attacker gained control, his massive arms wrapping around Eitan's neck in a deadly chokehold. Eitan fought back, struggling to free himself, but the strength of the thug was overwhelming. With his vision fading, Eitan was losing valuable time. He tried to put his forearm between the thug's arm and his neck. He tried to head-butt in reverse as a final attempt, which harmlessly bounced off his attacker's shoulder, resulting in a fatal error. With a sickening crack, the hooded man snapped Eitan's neck, his lifeless body crumpling to the floor.

Flechtheim stood frozen in horror, his heart pounding in his chest.

"Enough," the knife-wielding man barked in Arabic, his voice crisp and commanding.

The search for the painting began. Flechtheim watched helplessly as they tore apart his beloved flat. Following what seemed like a lifetime, they found it—a false panel behind the fireplace. The Woman in Red.

Without a word, the men wrapped the painting in a rug and disappeared into the night, leaving nothing but death and destruction in their wake.

Flechtheim's lifeless eyes stared at the ceiling, his heart having finally given out, just as they had planned.

CHAPTER 3

Berlin

He exited the subterranean metro world and emerged into the brisk night air of Berlin, across from his destination. No car park to scan, just a straight shot to the door with no government or local surveillance cameras. The smell came to him so rapidly that his nostrils flared as he opened the glass door, wet with condensation from the inside despite the weather averaging around twenty degrees Celsius outside. It smelled the same all over the world: men's sweat from exertion on the dojo floor. It didn't matter where he was in the world or how hard some of the upscale martial arts studios would perfume the air with air fresheners; there's no hiding the smell of the fear and excitement the body secretes when the adrenal glands kick in.

This location was adjoining to Wurgreengel, an upscale bar, and was a mixed martial arts center. Not his first choice for working out but based on his limited time between flights and his desire to stave off sleep from jet lag, he'd searched for martial arts on his handheld device, and this center had been the first one to come up.

He crossed the threshold into the acrid smell and approached the cast-iron front desk, where a heavily tattooed woman sat reading a popular magazine featuring celebrities' lifestyles and said in German, "Fifty euros."

She just glanced up at the broad-shouldered stranger, who responded in accented German, "One workout. Just today. From out of town."

She gave him a dismissive look. "Ten euros."

He reached into his pants pocket, extracted a ten-euro bill, and placed it on the top of the desk. He never quite understood the beliefs in many parts of the world of not handing over money into the receiving hand. It already had hundreds of germs on it regardless of whether you picked it up from the person's hand or a money-exchange dish. She took the money, informed him about the towels in the locker and including showers in the price, and returned to her magazine. He turned and walked around the perimeter of the dojo mat, looking straight ahead while scanning his surroundings with his eyes–counting heads, as they called it back in the days. Old habits die hard.

As he entered the even-worse-smelling locker room, he caught a handful of glances his way. Stashing his overnight bag in a locker, he retrieved his sweatpants and a long-sleeve t-shirt, failing to hide his well-built physique. He changed and secured his locker, placed the key in his pocket, grabbed a towel, and walked out onto the training floor. He spotted an open area that looked good for stretching.

He began with his feet apart about shoulder width and began neck circles while simultaneously stretching his fingers and wrists in clockwise and counterclockwise motions. Followed by some stretching with the towel to further increase his range of motion, pushing his body to the limit of flexibility.

Afterwards, he began the traditional katas, starting with the

Korean, followed by Japanese karate style, and ending with judo and aikido circular patterns, consuming twenty minutes of warmups. Only then did he walk over to the double-end bag: a highly efficient piece of equipment that is attached to the floor and ceiling by a rope with a small, round punching bag in the center, used by boxers mostly for timing and speed.

He began rhythmically jabbing and bobbing to an imaginary opponent, just breaking a sweat after six minutes of continuous hitting and reacting to the small bag coming at his face as it responded to his perfectly timed blows. He stopped and began doing some arm circles while slowing down his breathing when a young man in his late teens or early twenties approached him.

The young man spoke, unsure of himself, in German, "Sir, can you help hold these mitts for me?" His eyes never left his mitts, not wanting to look directly into the stranger's eyes for fear of rejection or shyness. The broad-shouldered stranger said nothing and reached out for the focus mitts. He placed them on each of his hands and walked further out onto the mat with the young man, assuming a fighting position his left hand higher and further forward than his right at face height, while the younger man began jabbing and crossing with his left hand and striking irregularly and clumsily with his right.

After about two minutes, the younger man's efforts exhausted him, and he placed his hands on his hips. The stranger took the opportunity to say, "You are leading with your head before you throw your jab, and your stance is too far forward when you hook with your lead hand. Here, let's try it again, and relax when you throw your punches."

He adjusted the young man's fighting guard position and

Each jab from the young man caused the American to take a slight step back. He recoiled a bit before his lead arm made contact. "Good. See, you got the hang of it."

Just then, a large military type, over six feet of muscle from head to toe, moved in, and the young man quickly retreated, fear etched on his face.

The larger man growled something that sounded like an eastern German dialect. "What is this? Are you a trainer or something, foreigner?" He stepped forward, blocking the young man's view of the stranger standing in front of him. The stranger knew a bully when he met one, and this ex-military or bouncer was just like others all over the world - looking to compensate for a lack of intelligence or manhood, whichever smaller.

The stranger just smiled, knowing that feigning ignorance of the rules of the gym would either defuse the situation or piss off the Neanderthal. At this point, neither mattered to him. Taking his time, he slid his hands out of the mitts and tossed them to the now frightened younger man.

"The young man wanted help with his form," he offered in German.

"And who are you to give it?" the heavier man said with a smile and a nod to his left. The stranger glanced over to see two other Middle Eastern men about the same size as the man approaching him. Nevertheless, he avoided drawing attention to himself because Berlin's airport was a popular hub for flights to the Middle East. He didn't want to burn his usage and reroute through a different European airport, adding hours to his flight times.

"Look, I was not aware of the rules. I am just traveling through. I will be gone in less than an hour."

"Oh, you think it's that easy, huh?" As the massive man placed his arms in front of his chest, the stranger noticed on the inside of the right forearm a tattoo of the German Special Forces Commando Division motto: Facit Omina Voluntas, the will is decisive.

From the looks of these two slabs of meat, they were worse than bullies; they were active duty, and not seeing any action, they wanted to pick on anyone for any excuse. Or they were terrible at blending in if they were part of a hit team. He thought the earlier; they were too amateurish in their approach.

"Look," began the stranger.

"Stop. You are hurting my ears with your German gibberish. Speak English, American asshole," the man growled down at him. The extra two circled around and behind the smaller man, closing the distance and making it a harder choice of options for him.

The classic schoolyard scenario played out around the world—except, with kids, there might be a bleeding nose or a few bruises. Here, extra-large grown men acting poorly would cause extra pain and broken bones rather than bruising.

The now-labeled American glanced around most of the dozen people who were working out but who stopped and were now staring at him in the center of these giants. Some with smiles on their faces, as if they had seen this type of harassment before from the regulars.

There is always a chance you will come across territorial

individuals, especially in mixed martial arts centers, where the people have less respect than in the traditional dojos that he preferred to work out at. In the same sense, mixed gyms offer more realistic fighting because, once you hit the ground, you will keep fighting with the grappling arts, like on the streets.

No one is going to let you tap out or break up a fight today, he thought. He gave a short exhale and flexed all his muscles in his back, arms, and legs for a brief second, firing up his nervous system, though most observers might not have noticed any change in the American's posture.

The broad-shouldered American said, in English this time, "Are you active?" The German just stared back at him, breathing harder, working himself up. So, the American switched to German again: "Are you serving? If so, then you will get the right care afterwards. If not, I would feel bad."

All three men began laughing as if he just told a joke. The instigator nodded his head a bit to the right, towards the man behind the American. They wanted to humiliate him primarily. If it was going to be a real throw down, they all wouldn't have been talking and standing around.

"Let me buy you guys a beer?" he tried again in German, sliding his left foot back but keeping his right foot forward and pointing inward. He shifted his weight a little more onto his back leg, keeping his arms by his sides and his hands open.

"Better yet, we take your money, tourist, and then we get our own beer," the larger man in front of him spoked in broken English, and he lunged at the American with his right fist as the two others reached for the man's arms by his side. This left him no option but to take the blow to the face, which would cause, most likely, a broken nose, possibly jaw, based on the extra-large size of the man's fist coming at him.

He'd already imagined this situation before their move, like a chess game, factoring in all the possibilities and responses to certain events before he reacted. A true counter-fighter is often in a better position than the attacker, allowing one's opponent to show their weakness first.

As the large man lunged, he kept his legs too close together, an amateur mistake allowing many possibilities for countering. Except there were two additional factors standing behind him with their own threats. They also made the classic blunder of using their size, thinking people naturally back down from them. They'd never thought through what might happen if someone actually put up a fight.

As the initial attacker's fist crossed the inner zone–the area between the elbows and chest in classic martial arts training–he was too close to kick, but just right for throwing or using an elbow or a knee strike.

The American chose the latter as the larger man's fist came only inches from his face and the additional two were grabbing his wrists. He slid his head to the right, allowing the larger man's fist to pass by, harmless to him but hitting the man's friend in the face instead, causing the man to release the American's wrist. Simultaneously, the American raised his left knee into the oncoming man's groin. The weight of the man was too much, and as he groaned from the strike, the American carried the larger man over with him onto the mat, pulling the additional attacker on top of them still holding onto the American's right wrist.

Anyone else would panic, with two people piled on top of them. Not the American. He went into automatic mode from years of training. Now down to two from three, so his odds just went up. The third held his mouth as blood dripped from it, and he backed off rather than engage since the other two were on top of their adversary.

The American took his free left hand and executed a ridge strike at the punching man's vertebral artery, between his thick neck and collarbone. He was further stunned, but he didn't move. The American followed up with a thumb strike, to the trachea of the man's throat. Causing the nerves in the man's throat to close down and creating a seizure-like reaction that left him unable to breathe.

The German rolled away, gasping for air and clenching his throat. He lay in a fetal position, dry heaving while trying to breathe.

The athletic stranger didn't wait. He struck out with his free left leg a round kick to the side of the man's temple while holding onto his right wrist, making a sickening whack sound causing the man's head to snap back, hit the mat, and jerk forward with a whiplash motion, overloading his neurological senses and rendering him unconscious.

The American jumped to a standing position and faced the man who had been punched in the face, realizing that this would not end as nicely as he planned out. He needed to end it and walk away.

Glancing behind himself, the American observed that the two assailants were still incapacitated. He walked towards the lockers, noticing for the first time the pounding heavy-metal music blaring. He heard the threat from behind once again.

The bloody-mouthed dark-skinned man pulled out a quick-release knife about six centimeters in length with his right hand and charged the American, quick and low, leading with his head and right shoulder and screaming obesities.

The American's reflexes were damn good. He didn't reach for the weapon and try to disarm the attacker. Instead, he slid sideways like a matador, allowing a bull to pass. Using the larger man's energy and inertia, the American extended his ki, or centralized energy, driving his opponent further into an uncontrollable motion of no return by placing a hand behind the larger man's shoulder and using a tankan aikido variation, pushing with force twice as powerful as the man's bodyweight would normally allow. But as the larger man went by, the American spun using the turning momentum and threw an elbow strike to the base of the man's neck with all his weight, falling on top of the man as they went to the ground.

The American moved into a karate front stance and delivered a second vicious blow with a reverse punch to the base of the man's rising head, knocking him unconscious.

Less than a few minutes after the encounter started, the foreigner moved toward the locker room to retrieve his belongings before the local police got involved. He realized time was critical and wanted to get out of there before anyone else felt like pounding on him. He exited through a side door but not before looking over at the younger man, who was still holding his mitts and giving him a smile and thumbs up as he walked out. Oh well, I burned this route for a while, and I didn't sign in, the American thought as he walked across the street and hopped onto a tram passing by and heading in the direction of the airport.

CHAPTER 4

King Fahd International Airport

The brand-new Mercedes-Benz S-Class sedan taxi pulled up to the monstrous bomb barrier that was two meters tall and as far as the eye could see and that had periodic openings near the departure gates for the French airline Ceil Bleu. Cars stacked five to six deep parallel to each other, bringing the entire traffic to one immense idle.

Mobs of people were pouring from their cars, weaving back and forth between stalled traffic and exiting as rapidly to the extent possible at the entrance. Many were exchanging farewells in the minimal amount of space. The driver of the Mercedes inched his way to the closest opening, which was still about ten meters from the nearest baggage check-in. He squeezed forward as far as he could, bringing his bumper close to the van parked in front of him, filled with goats and children. On top a pile of luggage, stacked one meter high. When the Mercedes stopped, a package fell from the untethered mass, and then the owner yelled for help as all the luggage and boxes followed, falling to the ground all around his vehicle and on top of the hood of the Mercedes. As children and goats dispersed like a well-rehearsed fire drill, they began gathering their belongings and animals, bringing the almost not moving traffic to a complete standstill.

This provoked calls of anger from drivers who already

dropped off their passengers and were eager to get away from the terminal to pick up their upcoming customer. No one angrier at the van owner than the driver of the Mercedes, who leaped out of his car and began yelling in rapid Arabic at the dumbfounded man standing with a goat in one arm and juggling boxes in the other.

Two large, stern-looking men in blue uniforms from a security team, both carrying LSAT light machine guns, approached the van without caution and began encouraging the man to get his belongings in order and to get going before his vehicle and his contraband were impounded and he, his kids, all of them had to walk back to the village they came from.

The passenger of the Mercedes thought this was an ideal fortunate opportunity to leave the taxi without being noticed, as everyone's attention focused on the commotion occurring in front of his car. He handed the driver an American fifty-dollar bill. Still worth something in these parts of the world. The driver thanked him profusely and offered his deepest apology for his delay and wished his passenger great joy and prosperity in the future. The traveler thought, *how true*, as he opened and shut his door before the driver completed his sentence.

As the man stepped from the car, onto the curb and into the blazing sunlight, he felt goosebumps ripple across his forearms as his body tried to adjust from the cool interior of the Mercedes to the unbearable sizzling heat from the midday sun. The man thought, *and this is winter here?*

The man's sole possession was an expensive messenger bag, with room for a laptop and a couple of changes of clothing and additional necessities. He wore an Anderson and Sheppard tailored suit from 11 St. George Street on Saville Row. Including a tie, despite the temperature reaching over 120 degrees Fahrenheit. He shaved and wore round-rim glasses with clear plastic lenses, enhancing the entire persona he was trying to portray, despite having perfect eyesight. He dressed for attention as an important and wealthy business executive to be taken seriously and with respect rather than trying to blend in with the rest of the Middle Eastern passengers, or so he thought.

He was being paid a sizable sum to perform this task, and it would keep him in good standing with his benefactors and, more importantly, the lifestyle he became accustomed to while living abroad in Europe, especially Paris. He loved the French city the most, with its excellent dining, cultural events, and passionate debates with fellow intellects—which is how he thought of himself with his recent master's degree in biblical archeology, specifically the geological history of Palestine—and, of course, his favorite reason for being in the City of Lights: The French women.

He stepped forward into the queue for the airline, behind a familiar mishap of a scene of travelers, to wait through the mundane, extended, zigzag pattern the security enforced. Unlike the large amusement parks in the West, where they entertain while waiting in the queue, this ferreted out anyone looking for trouble. He used a mental game that he played since he was a little child to calm his nerves.

He usually observes a person standing seven people ahead of himself and then pick a destination on the outbound flights displayed overhead. Then count seven down from the top. Once he found the flight, he then mathematically multiplied the first number of the departing time with the number seven and then divided that number by the arrival time. The longer the equation took, the better. He remains focused and does not draw attention to himself, acting nerdish and harmless even though being Middle Eastern, young, and fit the search and question profile. That was why they chose him for the task: his authentic behavior.

As the man approached the final and fifth checkpoint, forty-five minutes after entering the queue, he handed over his passport, work visa, hotel bill where he stayed the past three nights, and a special yellow government contact slip given to foreigners, with privileges that went with it.

The ticket handler merely glanced up to check that the photo id looked remotely like the person standing before him. Homegrown terrorism was not much of a concern in these parts of the world. They were letting them out of their country to play havoc with the rest of the world, or so they thought. Besides, by the fifth identity challenge in line, most common criminals would have broken the queue based purely on redundancy. Most people usually possess a sense of guilt for doing something wrong and fear of being searched.

"Designation?" asked the board security officer with the paperwork in hand.

"Paris," the man replied. He never stopped his mathematical calculations of the flight numbers. His eyes showed no dilation, rapid blinking, or avoidance for that matter during the officer's fifteen-second assessment of him, though being one of the most sought-after men in the world, a person of interest for multiple government and criminal organizations alike.

"Line one," the officer said in English with a hint of a Sudanese accent.

The man thought, And the world is becoming a smaller place indeed, as he walked towards the bins to place his belongings to pass through the x-ray machines.

Unrushed, he removed his shoes from his feet and placed them in a bin. After, he placed his messenger bag onto the conveyor belt, remembering not to place it in a bin. A new rule that no one understood or cared about; they just wanted to get it over with and be on their way to the airport lounge.

He slid his watch off as he removed his suit jacket and folded it in half. Next his belt and placed it on top and into the awaiting bin. All that remained was to walk through the old-fashioned metal detector with his passport and ticket in hand. The truth is, they were indifferent, the kingdom's oil supply ensured continued loyalty, preventing any uprisings against the royal family. Every male received four thousand euros per month for living in the same place all their lives. There were no restrictions on traveling, and visitors came and went without difficulties. There were always new infrastructure projects being built, and old ones torn down regardless of their age, all in the name of progress and keeping the kingdom running smoothly.

He just completed his mathematical equation as the x-ray machine conveyor belt stopped with his bag in view on the large flat screen monitor above. Several security personnel became aroused and moved closer to the screen to look. After a lot of pointing and puffing out of chests in pride at their discovery, one approached the man, who had, during the distraction, placed his shoes, belt, and suit jacket back on and clamp on his watch.

"Sir is this your carry-on bag?" inquiry the security agent, now staring at the well-dressed man with interest.

The man smiled broadly, revealing his overly white and straight dental work he'd had done in Paris by one of the top professionals' money could buy. "Yes, it is. Why do you ask?"

No one questions security unless they are looking for trouble or are of higher placement in society or think as much. The man's tone and mannerism presented to the guard a dilemma he had not approached before. If the well-dressed, Western-style man before him was of the royal family or supporting workforce, he would be in lots of trouble. He'd just sat through an extensive briefing on the latest reports on stolen artifacts in the Middle East and heading through Europe, and what he thought he'd seen on the screen looked ancient indeed.

CHAPTER 5

7:00 Am Louver Museum

Torrential rains occurred for ten days straight in central and northeastern France. The news anchor continued such a historical event that has not taken place since the early 1900s, when over 40 people died along the Seine and forced thousands to evacuate. "It was 1910 to be correct you dumb bitch" muttered Monsieur Chartrand, staring at the television for a moment before walking out of the changing room for workers of the Louve Museum. Few workers chuckled nervously at Monsieur Chartrand's comment. None added they were all tired working around the clock to preserve the threatened artwork stored in Paris' most celebrated museum. The substantial rains caused the Seine in Paris to rise to 18 feet by Thursday evening, flooding the lower embankments and shutting several roads. Water became too far above considered safe to the museum's lower-level viewing halls. They decided to cancel all vacations and bring in extra workers to assist with moving the pieces to higher grounds. To add insult to injury, they still were preparing for the special dignitary coming in two nights' time for a special viewing. The real reason for the event remained a secret to almost everyone.

After the Second World War and the disgrace of the German mad man who stole artworks from around the world. The detailed records kept by the Germans gave the serial numbers and family names of rightful ownership of the works. Most were killed or went underground for their own safety many years after the war. The origin country received the arts that were not claimed first. After many disputes and court cases of false claims of ownership and years of tied up in court cases. Certain works disappeared over night, not to be seen in public for decades. It wasn't until someone died that their undiscovered works hit the headlines.

Those who knew kept the whereabouts of most pieces a secret all along. Or at least they liked to think they did. Then several curators gathered in Paris, then Germany, and followed with Italy to split up the pieces and bring them to public viewing once again. Of course, the financial incentive for many pieces to be given up by their modern-day owners worked for a few. Others mysteriously were gone, along with their manors and estates from surprise fires. The infighting needed to stop, with the bloodshed. So, the main curators sent their deputy curator out to negotiate the exchange of works. Many didn't want to give them up without large compensation. The results were private benefactors putting up millions as a loan for the museum to display along with paying them interest on the loans of such stated works. That was not enough when the Asian and Arabs got wind of these deals. The Russians threatened military action over a certain painting unless they had initial bid rights. Thus, arriving at the present-day event. Country's curators picked their top sponsors, so to speak, to enter the evening like a prize fighter and try to outbid each other for some. It would be name recognition with their family named to a certain hall or an entire museum. People considered it as the embodiment of ugly capitalism at its best. What no one could imagine being more profitable was to retake the artwork again after the sales, until now.

CHAPTER 6

7:30 AM – Louvre Museum, Sub Basement

Abdel's shift was supposed to be over. After a grueling night, the cool, damp air of the Louvre's sub basement only heightened his exhaustion. As he trudged down the narrow corridor, the air weighed heavy with the scents of damp stone and old marble, mingling with the earthy musk of ancient artifacts. Lost in thought that he almost didn't notice the footsteps until a snapped finger jolted him.

"You there! Give us a hand," snapped an officer from the exhibits team, his voice echoing sharply against the stone walls.

Abdel clenched his jaw. His French was passable, but the tone was unmistakable—these aristocratic types had little patience for those they saw as outsiders. Glancing down the hall, he noticed two men struggling to maneuver a smaller yet still weighty replica of the Winged Victory of Samothrace. The smaller statue, crafted from the same grey-white marble as the original, is an homage to the ancient masterpiece, its presence a piece of history in itself. The team moved it into the hallway in a rush, leaving it blocking the passage as they worked to repair a wall that had cracked from recent flooding.

Abdel approached, feeling the officer's impatient gaze. As they tried to lift the statue onto a wooden crate, the officer began to pace, his eyes darting between the struggling men and the exposed, delicate stone.

"Careful! One slip, and we're all out of a job—or worse," he barked, his voice taut with concealed anxiety.

The officer, growing increasingly frustrated, eventually pitched in, though his physical contribution was limited. Sweat darkened his shirt as he pushed against the marble, grunting with each attempt. With a collective heave, they settled the statue onto the crate. The men straightened up, catching their breath, their muscles aching. The officer pulled a handkerchief from his pocket to wipe his face, oblivious as a pair of key cards slipped out and skidded under the crate.

"That's enough. You can go now," he said, dismissing the men with a wave.

Abdel turned to leave, his eyes lingering on the key cards barely visible under the crate. The officer's mobile buzzed, and he raised it to his ear with a huff. "What now?" he muttered, his words laden with irritation. "Oui?" he snapped, already pivoting toward the stairs, his focus shifting to whatever new crisis awaited him above.

Halfway up the stairwell, he received a new instruction over the phone: the elevator had broken down, and every artifact in the sub basement needed covering until maintenance could repair the cracked wall. He cursed again, casting a glance over his shoulder.

"You! Wait!" His voice echoed down the hall as he called out to Abdel, who hoped to slip away unnoticed.

Abdel stood still, eyes fixed on the departing men, leaving him alone in the officer's crosshairs. "Oui, Monsieur?"

The officer's brow furrowed with impatience. "I need you to cover everything with tarps. Make sure nothing gets damaged by dust or debris. Understand?"

Abdel nodded, his exhaustion mounting. "Oui, Monsieur," he replied, fighting to keep his tone respectful. He couldn't afford to lose this job; his family relied on every paycheck he sent home.

Without another word, the officer disappeared up the stairs, his footsteps fading as Abdel watched, resignation settling over him. With a sigh, he returned to the corridor, scanning the cluttered space filled with centuries-old artifacts. He spotted the stack of tarps and ropes at the end of the hall, a grim reminder of the hours of work still ahead. The thought of missing the football game at Le Comptoir with his friends gnawed at him. They'd planned to meet up, maybe even hit Le Café des Sports later, where the thrum of a live DJ can drown out the week's drudgery.

Just as he reached for a tarp, a glint of something under the crate caught his eye. The officer's key cards.

Abdel hesitated, glancing around to ensure no one was watching. He crouched down, his fingers stretching as he strained to reach the cards. His arm wouldn't fit, and frustration mounted as he searched for something to help. His gaze landed on the rope. He tied a makeshift knot at one end and looped it under the crate, trying to snag the cards.

The voices of men echoed from the stairwell. Abdel's pulse spiked, and he fumbled with the rope, his hands slick with sweat as the footsteps grew louder. The cards slipped just out of reach, mocking his efforts. With a quick glance over his shoulder, he flattened himself against the cold tile, the rope trembling in his grip as he made one final, desperate attempt.

The cards jerked free with a sudden pull, landing just within his reach. Abdel snatched them, stuffing them into his pocket as he scrambled to his feet. His heart thundered, and he struggled to catch his breath as a group of workers appeared at the end of the hall, too absorbed in their conversation to notice him. They gave him only a cursory glance, too preoccupied discussing a beautiful woman they'd seen in the reception hall.

He exhaled slowly, relief washing over him. In his pocket, the cards possessed a cool, heavy feel, a mystery he hadn't expected to find at the end of a thankless shift. He wasn't sure what he'd do with them or if he'd even dare use them, but their presence stirred something within him—an opportunity he hadn't yet grasped.

Pushing the thoughts aside, he returned to his task, covering the artifacts with practiced efficiency, his movements quick and deliberate. The officer would be back soon, and the last thing Abdel needed was another run-in. But the feel of the cards in his pocket lingered, a quiet thrill breaking through the fog of his exhaustion.

As he tied down the final tarp, he caught his reflection in the dusty glass of a display case. He looked tired, worn down by extensive hours and thankless tasks. But tonight, as he walked back up those stairs, he did so with a newfound sense of purpose. Whatever secrets those cards held, they were his now—and maybe, just maybe, they would lead him to something further than the daily grind that had come to define his life.

CHAPTER 7

Hauptbahnhof, Berlin

The American moved with precision, hopping on and off the trams, each stop calculated as part of his counter-surveillance routine. For thirty minutes, he studied the faces around him—glasses, hats, purses—each detail committed to memory. Old tradecraft never died, no matter the city or the mission. A dance every operative knew, a matter of survival. Some performed it better than others. His heart pounded, adrenaline flooding his veins, but now it was tapering off, leaving him drenched in sweat. Despite wanting to shower, time did not permit it. He needed to get to the locker—the one with his bug-out bag. A field necessity when your only home base is an ever-shifting shadow.

Slipping through an unmarked service door at Berlin's Hauptbahnhof, he ducked his head just enough to avoid the cameras. He blended into the crowd like a ghost, moving up the escalator, eyes sweeping the vast expanse of the station. He scanned for anything out of place—anyone out of sync with the steady rhythm of the commuters.

He headed for the least convenient section of the terminal, the kind of spot no one willingly approached. His hand found the well-worn key in his pocket. The tiny locker not larger than a shoebox, scarred with years of dents and scuffs—a perfect hiding spot because it hadn't drawn attention in years. He crouched low and slid the key into the lock, noting with satisfaction that the metal remained just as he'd left it. No fresh scratches. No recent repairs.

A battered brown paper bag inside bound tightly by a weathered rubber band. He glanced around, catching a quick glimpse of the ceiling, reassuring himself that no new cameras had been installed. His fingers worked fast, unfolding the bag to reveal a handkerchief embroidered with the initials "MS." Tucked within a small key. He palmed it, eyes narrowing as he refolded the handkerchief and stashed it back in the locker. The routine was second nature, but the tension in his shoulders never eased.

Moving two rows over, closer to an emergency exit, he slid the new key into a taller locker. Inside, a duffel bag, a backpack, and a briefcase awaited him. Hanging alongside them were a selection of outerwear—a windbreaker, rain jacket, and a winter coat—all in the latest styles, all blue.

He grabbed the duffel and locked the door with a practiced efficiency. Ten seconds flat. He made his way to the men's washroom, moving with purpose, slipping into a stall and nudging the toilet lid closed with his foot. Cleanliness wasn't a given, no matter how precise the Germans were.

He stripped off his shirt and hooked the duffel on the door, unzipping it to reveal the fresh contents within. A crisp, extra-large Boss dress shirt in navy, freshly pressed. He laid it on the hook, pulling out khaki slacks and a belt. Chestnut-brown Fleishman shoes, buffed to perfection, followed by dark brown socks.

Then came a tan sports jacket with hidden pockets, the kind that might resemble a techie's over-designed vest but far more subtle. He slid out 1,000 Swiss francs and 400 euros, tucking the bills into a money clip and then into his right pocket. Perfect for avoiding pickpockets. They'd never know what hit them if they tried. The rise in cross-border pickpocketing had been a silent epidemic since the Schengen Agreement opened doors for petty thieves to move freely from country to country.

Reaching into the bag, he activated an electric razor. It wasn't ideal, but it ought to do the trick. A quick shave, not a perfect one—enough to pass as a harried businessman, rushing between meetings.

The final detail: one of the two passports concealed in his jacket. The fabric of the jacket was a synthetic marvel, designed to trick airport scanners into thinking a tear had been hastily sewn up. He doubted most security guards would give it a second glance. He opened the United States passport and smiled faintly at the name inside: R. Stone, Chicago, Illinois.

In under ten minutes, he stepped out of the restroom, freshly dressed and blending back into the flow of travelers. He approached the ticket counter and bought a business-class seat to Bern, Switzerland. Almost perfect—just a businessman returning from a trip. Bern being his gateway, a place to restock, blend in, and then disappear. From there, a flight to the Middle East awaited.Switzerland remained a hub for the global elite including wealthy Middle Easterners all too eager to visit their favorite Swiss bankers. He vanished into the crowd, his mission far from over, the world none the wiser.

CHAPTER 8

The Train

The first nine hours of the ten-hour train journey passed without incident. Stone reclined in his first-class seat, feigning rest while his eyes remained closed, but his senses were attuned to every sound and movement around him remaining razor-sharp. The overpowering scent of his seatmate- a woman who seemed to have bathed in cheap perfume- kept him alert. Thankfully, she hadn't attempted conversation. In fact, she'd given him a once-over with a disdainful glare before turning away and falling into a deep, snoring sleep that lasted the entire ride.

Feeling the urge to stretch his legs, Stone carefully maneuvered around his dozing seatmate, stepping into the aisle without disturbing her. The carriage filled with weary travelers- some dozing, a small number absorbed in newspapers. A few with laptops open but seemed more interested in the passing scenery than their screens. It was that lull in the journey where time seemed to stretch, and travelers let their guards down—a mistake he couldn't afford.

He made his way toward the dining car, curious whether the cuisine would be palatable Swiss fare or hearty German delights. As he walked, he kept his gaze forward, but his peripheral vision swept over faces and body language. The savory aroma of Älplermagronen—a rich gratin of potatoes, macaroni, cheese, cream, onions, and stewed apple—wafted through the corridor. Tempting, but far too heavy for his current state. Just as he contemplated alternative options, a subtle movement caught his eye.

A woman in her mid-thirties stood near the entrance to the dining car. Blonde hair grazed her shoulders, framing strikingly cool blue eyes. Dressed in dark slacks and a matching sweater rolled up to her elbows, she might have seemed like any other traveler. But the athletic watch on her wrist and the pronounced musculature of her forearms hinted at something else. A brief eye contact occurred between them—a flicker of recognition in hers, followed by a minute twitch of her facial muscles. She lowered her left elbow toward her hip before pulling down her sleeves, a classic tell of someone concealing a firearm.

Too late to hide, sweetheart, Stone thought. Whether she recognized him or marked him as a person of interest didn't matter. He continued into the dining car, maintaining his pace. Turning back now would be a dead giveaway. Jumping off the train wasn't an option, either. Questions swirled in his mind: How had they picked up his trail? Blind luck, or had there been a leak? No time for that. He needed to assess how many were involved and formulate a plan to neutralize the threat without causing a scene.

CHAPTER 9

Dinning Car

He didn't wait long. As he walked into the dining car, a meticulously dressed maître d' greeted him with a smile befitting a five-star hotel. "Good evening, sir. Joining us for an early dinner?" he asked in polished English.

"Ein Tisch für eine Person, bitte," Stone replied in German, requesting a table for one.

The maître d' bowed and led him to a table on the right side, near the small bar with a panoramic view of the mountainous countryside. "Möchten Sie eine Weinkarte sehen?" he inquired— would you like to see a wine list?

Stone shook his head politely, adjusting his seat to keep the entrance within his line of sight. The maître d' bowed again and departed as two servers appeared, setting a bottle of water on the table and presenting the day's menu.

Before Stone could pursue it, two hulking men entered the car. Their chiseled jaws and muscular builds reminded him of the thugs he'd dispatched at the dojo earlier. They brushed past the staff, planting themselves on bar stools—conveniently leaving the one closest to Stone vacant. Their sport jackets hung open, intentionally revealing shoulder holsters on their left sides. The ill-fitting clothes did little to conceal the bulge of their firearms. Professional, perhaps, but their restless movements betrayed discomfort. The bartender approached to take their order but hesitated as they stared intently at Stone, hands resting conspicuously on their thighs.

The atmosphere in the dining car grew tense. Patrons exchanged uneasy glances, sensing the undercurrent of hostility. If this were an assassination, they'd have made their move already. No, they were waiting—for orders, for backup, for something. Stone surmised a third party orchestrating this play.

Patience will be required of the muscular twins, he mused. Any sudden moves on his part might trigger an immediate response. Instead, he decided to proceed as if unconcerned. After all, he was genuinely hungry. In fluent German, he ordered Zürcher Geschnetzeltes, substituting chicken for the traditional pork and requesting a lighter vegetable or tomato base instead of the heavy cream sauce. His request for iced tea raised an eyebrow but elicited no comment. The server nodded, collecting the menu.

As the waiter turned, he nearly collided with the blonde woman from earlier. She extended her hand gracefully, accepting the menu and allowing the waiter to pull out the chair across from Stone. Without waiting for an invitation, she sat down, crossing her legs and draping a linen napkin over her lap. She glanced up at the waiter. "Ein Glas Rotwein, bitte," she ordered—a glass of red wine.

"Do you mind?" she asked Stone, her English tinged with an accent he couldn't place.

"Not at all. Fine dining is best enjoyed with pleasant company," he replied smoothly.

A brief look out the window preceded her locking eyes with

him, a faint smile playing on her lips. "Aren't we getting ahead of ourselves, Dr. Stone?"

"You seem to have me at a disadvantage, Miss...?"

"Eis," she declared, the German word for 'ice.'

Fitting, Stone thought. Cold and potentially lethal. "Well then, Miss Eis, to what do I owe the pleasure?"

Her smile didn't reach her eyes. "Your charm might work on others, but not on me," she said, taking a sip of the wine just delivered to the table. "You're a person of interest regarding matters in Berlin. I'm here to escort you back for questioning."

Stone stirred his iced tea thoughtfully, fishing out a packet of real sugar from the assortment of sweeteners—a rarity these days amid artificial substitutes. "Don't you mean 'we'?" he asked, nodding subtly toward the two enforcers at the bar who were watching them intently.

She glanced over her shoulder dismissively. "Them? Mere window dressing. I assured my superiors you're a reasonable man. There's nowhere for you to go, and no logical reason to make this difficult."

She pushed her wine glass forward. Stone caught subtle notes of earth and perhaps rose—a complex blend. "You haven't told me what the charges are. Isn't that standard procedure in law enforcement?" he queried, taking a deliberate sip of his tea. The cool beverage being a welcome contrast to the heat of the unfolding situation.

"Interpol has its protocols," she replied cryptically, her smile twisting ever so slightly. She adjusted her posture, her calf brushing against his leg beneath the table—a calculated move.

Through the window, Stone noticed the train approaching a series of tunnels carved into the Swiss mountains. Passengers seemed oblivious, engrossed in their meals or conversations. He estimated they had about ten minutes before entering the primary tunnel—a window of opportunity.

Their meals arrived with less fanfare than the wine service. Stone picked up his knife and fork, cutting into the tender chicken. "If you don't mind, it's been a long day," he said, savoring a bite.

"By all means," she gestured elegantly. "They say a condemned man should enjoy his last meal, yes?" Without waiting for a response, she leaned over and deftly speared a piece of chicken from his plate, bringing it to her lips. "Not bad for train cuisine," she remarked, licking her lips.

Confident to the point of arrogance, Stone noted. The tension at the bar had lessened; the two brutes seemed almost relaxed now, lulled by the facade of a civil dinner. Underestimating me—rookie mistake.

The shadows outside deepened as the train began its ascent into the mountains. Stone laid his knife to the left of his plate in a nonchalant manner, drawing her attention. He reached for his spoon to stir his drink, his movements measured. Her eyes flicked from the knife to his, a flash of realization dawning too late.

"Speaking of formalities, may I see some identification?" he asked innocently.

Her composure wavered for a brief moment. The train plunged into darkness as it entered the tunnel, the sudden absence of light engulfing the dining car. It would take at least fifteen seconds for the automatic systems to activate the interior lights—an energy-saving feature of the new Euro trains.

Fifteen seconds of darkness. More than enough time.

CHAPTER 10

Tunnel Vision

The train's dining car plunged into darkness. One or two passengers paused their conversations, but most carried on, used to the erratic electrical flickers on this route. Stone, however, was already on edge. The woman seated, who claimed to be with Interpol, began uncrossing her legs. Stone stood; his body taut with instinct. Later, he would replay this moment, sleepless in the dead of night, wondering if his actions were justified. But now, his survival depended on speed.

Doubt clouded his mind. Might she indeed be Interpol? They were approaching Bern, mere kilometers from the mountains where Stone hiked countless times. His hand closed around the cool metal of a spoon on the table. Without hesitation, his left hand delivered a palm strike to the blonde's forehead, a calculated blow being powerful yet not lethal—just in case she was telling the truth.

She gave out a short gasp, her eyes fluttering as darkness claimed her. She crumpled, tipping her chair backward, arms flailing helplessly. Stone had already begun to move. The rudimentary hulking man leapt from his stool as the woman's limp body collided with him. Stone's elbow shot up in a vicious arc, connecting with the man's chin. The massive man staggered, his bulk colliding into his partner.

Stone saw the second man's hand dart inside his jacket. Gun. Stone lunged, his left hand striking again—this time a brutal backfist to the man's temple. The man reached for Stone's arm, but the spoon was already swinging toward his ear. The scream that followed reverberated through the dining car, the man clutching his head in agony.

Dropping the spoon, Stone bolted toward the door. The rest of the passengers sat frozen in stunned silence, trying to comprehend the violence they'd just witnessed. Stone sprinted through the train cars, dodging the occasional groggy traveler, heart pounding in rhythm with his feet. With minimal pause, he took his duffel bag from the top of the sleeping woman., flinging it over his shoulder and continuing his dash toward the front of the train.

Behind him, the two dazed men recovered, guns drawn. They shoved past the bewildered staff and passengers, moving swiftly in pursuit.

Stone reached the final car, just before the supply and engineer cars. The conductor staff began their rounds, waking passengers, oblivious to the chaos that trailed behind Stone. They didn't see the broad-shouldered figure barging through the door until he was already inside, knocking two of them into their seats. A loud crack rang out— A bullet whizzed past Stone's head, lodging in the metal wall.

With a powerful kick, Stone slammed the door shut, locking it. Three wide-eyed staff members cowered before him, too terrified to speak. He didn't have time to offer reassurances. He reached for the emergency brake, hearing the desperate screams from the older men: "No!"

The brake engaged with a shudder, and for a moment, nothing happened. Then, a violent jolt threw everyone against the locked door. Stone knew the train wouldn't come to a full stop. but he needed every edge he could get. As the alarms blared, he ripped open the emergency exit, feeling the wind howl through the gap.

Stone placed a foot at the door's edge, grabbed an oversized duffel bag used for dirty linens and his own bag both placed in front of himself, offered the terrified men a wink, and hurled himself into the dark, roaring abyss. The door slammed shut behind him, and he vanished.

The men scrambled to their feet just as the gunmen burst into the car, weapons raised. "Wo ist der Mann?" the larger of the two growled, his eyes wild, scanning the room.

The trembling staff pointed toward the exit door, where the wind still howled outside. The train, brakes screeching, continued its relentless course down the tracks, trying in vain to slow the weight of metal and momentum.

CHAPTER 11

The Innkeeper

The sensation of falling seemed endless until the harsh impact of earth slammed into Stone's body. The wind was knocked from his lungs as he hit the dirt, a wave of dust enveloping him. Before he recovered, the force of the passing train caught him, tossing him another several meters. He tumbled, rolling to his feet with a groan, pain radiating from his ribs and leg.

The duffel bags absorbed some of the fall, and the adrenaline kept him moving. Sore but alive, Stone hobbled off the embankment, his eyes scanning the distant lights of a village less than a kilometer away. A narrow hiking path beckoned, offering a much-needed escape route. Stone gritted his teeth, limping down the path, putting ample distance between him and the speeding train.

With a quick glance, the innkeeper at the only inn in the village slid a key across the counter to him. Her hands busy kneading dough for the morning bread. No payment was necessary here—unlike the fancier hotels in Bern. Exhausted beyond words, Stone mumbled a thank you in German and made his way down the narrow hallway to the furthest room on the left. He collapsed onto the bed without undressing, letting sleep claim him in an instant.

Hours later, he awoke to the sound of raised voices outside

his window. Disoriented, Stone shook the cobwebs from his mind and moved cautiously to peer out. Two uniformed men argued with the innkeeper, their faces tense with suspicion.

"Frau, reports say a dangerous man jumped from a train this morning. We've searched every building except yours," one officer insisted, his tone a mix of frustration and urgency.

"Do I look like the sort to hide fugitives?" the innkeeper snapped back. "I have bread to bake, not criminals to hide."

The older officer's shoulders sagged in defeat, and after a small number added feeble protests, he and his partner retreated. As they disappeared down the road, the former Chief Justice Margaret shut the inn door and let out a laugh so loud that Stone nearly jumped out of his skin.

The innkeeper, once again busy with her dough, didn't notice Stone's silent approach as he entered the kitchen. When she at last looked up, she placed a hand on her chest, startled. "Good lord, you move like a ghost! You look even worse now than when you arrived—like a man running from something."

She stopped kneading for a moment, her eyes scanning his face. "I remember you from your last visit. You were quiet then too. Always off hiking in the mountains."

Stone gave a small nod, grateful for her discretion but knowing he couldn't stay.

Every move, every decision was calculated. It was how he survived up to this point, and why he was still breathing.

"I hope I haven't caused you trouble," in a measured voice.

She waved a hand, dismissing the thought. "Those boys

won't stay long. They'll watch for a bit, get bored, and move on."

If I let them, Stone thought. He could lure them into the woods, handle the situation. But the Justices granted him sanctuary. For now, it was best to remain the ghost they believed him to be.

"You're not a coffee drinker, are you?" she asked, turning to set a kettle on the stove. "Black tea?"

"That'll be fine. Thank you." Green tea was his preference, but he wasn't about to quibble over details.

"I'll make you something to eat. You should shower. You look like you've been dragged in from a storm." Her eyes ran over him, appraising, like a stray cat that wandered in.

"There are extra spare clothes the previous guest left behind may fit you, if you like"

"Much appreciated," he said, offering a small nod.

After a scalding shower and a shave, Stone emerged dressed in fresh khakis and a button-down shirt. Soft thuds echoed from his hiking boots on the wooden dining room floor.

Laughter drifted from the adjacent room.

"Oh, Cindy, this is Mr...?" The innkeeper's voice carried.

"Stone," he stated, stepping forward. "Nice to meet you, Cindy."

Her blue eyes flicked to his, calculating. Shoulder-length blonde hair framed her face, it was her watchful stance that caught Stone's attention—bureaucratic and keen. She was fit, mid-thirties maybe, dressed casually but alert, every movement precise.

"Guete Abig. Good evening," she greeted in Swiss German. Her handshake was firm but distant, her smile guarded.

Stone returned the greeting in near-flawless French. "Not at all, speak whichever language you prefer."

Cindy's smile sharpened. "May I practice my English with you?"

He nodded, settling into the chair across from her. This wasn't a conversation. More like an interrogation.

"So, Mr. Stone, what brings you to our small village?"

"On my way to Bern," Stone replied evenly. "I've enjoyed my stays here before. Quiet, no fuss." He let his eyes drift to her watch, a sleek and expensive Swiss model, before meeting her gaze again. Unmarried, no ring—but something told him there was further to this woman.

She laughed, a short, clipped sound. "A true American cowboy. Let me guess—Texas?"

Her eyes flicked down to his hands, noticing the calluses, the strong build of his palms. A slow, deliberate smile spread across her face. She wasn't one to be underestimated, and she was making sure he knew it.

Stone curled his fingers, retreating from the challenge. "How's the weather? Expecting rain?"

"No, clear skies. But storms can sneak up from the north."

The innkeeper chimed in, "Why don't you let Cindy take you to the train station? Mr. Gunterger will talk your ear off for hours if you run into him."

The police, Stone thought. This was a warning. The Justice was letting him know—there were eyes everywhere.

Cindy glanced at him, a question in her gaze. "I didn't know he still ran the shop," she said, probing.

"He'll never let his son handle it alone," the innkeeper waved dismissively. "Cindy, you'll drive Mr. Stone, won't you?"

Reluctantly, Cindy nodded, her posture stiff.

Stone noticed her unease right away. "That's okay. I don't want to impose."

The innkeeper's tone sharpened. "No imposition. You'll leave today. I've got a full house tomorrow."

Cindy's brow furrowed. Something was off. The innkeeper rarely had guests, let alone a full house.

Stone returned to his room, left 200 Swiss francs on the nightstand—far more than what was owed—but he owed her in other ways. When he returned to the entrance, Cindy stood there, hands on her hips, car keys in hand.

"Ready," she said, tight-lipped.

"Yes, thank you," he replied, extending his hand to the innkeeper. But instead of shaking it, she stepped forward and hugged him, her small frame just reaching his chest.

"Next time, call ahead," her eyes sparkling with a knowing wink. "I'll have the same room ready."

As they walked toward the road, Cindy's mood shifted abruptly. "If you think I'm leaving a fugitive in my village, you're mistaken."

Stone froze, taken aback. Her sudden shift was jarring, the tension palpable.

"Pardon? Maybe it's best we part ways here."

"Not a chance," she said, her stance widening, preparing for a fight. "You're coming with me to Bern, or I'll call the police."

Stone raised his hands in surrender. "Okay, okay. You want to cuff me now or wait until we get to the station?"

"What?" she snapped, confusion mingling with frustration. "Just get in the car. Put your bag in the boot."

Stone complied, noting the emptiness of the trunk. At least there's nothing suspicious there. He climbed into the front seat, and before he buckled his seatbelt, the Audi roared to life, speeding off down the narrow road.

This drive was going to be anything but peaceful.

CHAPTER 12

The Drive

Stone glanced over at Cindy, now hidden behind oversized sunglasses that obscured most of her face. She was a mystery, even more so as they hurtled down the road, the speedometer pushing 80 kilometers per hour. The small village square blurred past, unsettling the locals enjoying their midday meals, including two police officers whose heads snapped toward the car.

Cindy's lips curled into a subtle smile as she caught their shocked expressions in the rearview mirror.

"I'm surprised you don't get ticketed driving like this," Stone said, keeping his tone casual.

"They wouldn't dare," she replied, her voice flat, offering nothing additional.

For the next hour, they drove through winding roads carved out of the mountainous terrain, dipping and climbing through what once must have been impassable land. The beauty persisted, even with breakneck speed, though Stone kept his focus on her rather than the landscape. He wanted to know more about this woman—what she wasn't saying.

From the final ridge, the city of Bern appeared on the horizon. Twenty minutes, maybe less.

"Where did you train?" Stone asked a simple question, but

the tone carried weight.

Cindy didn't respond immediately. They were overtaking an 18-wheeler on a blind curve, the cliff's edge dangerously close. The truck driver laid on his horn, the sound reverberating through the narrow pass, Cindy showed almost no reaction.

"What are you talking about?" she shot back, her tone more accusatory than curious.

"Back at the inn," Stone continued, unbothered by her coldness. "Your stance—it had the precision of someone who's trained. Fencing, maybe?"

A short laugh escaped her lips, sharp and humorless. "Do you use that line with all the women you meet?" She glanced at him for a brief moment before pulling into a tight bend, the car handling the curve with terrifying ease. Her eyes never left the road.

Stone dealt with enough people in power to recognize the signs—a need to assert control, a hunger for dominance, male or female. Cindy being no different. She thrived on it.

"You were born into money," Stone observed, his tone calm but probing. "Top private schools. Trained in the refined arts—horseback riding, cricket... fencing."

For a considerable time, she didn't speak, but Stone could feel the tension rise with the car's speed as they descended the hill. She was testing him, pushing the limits.

"I hated riding," she at last said, her voice tight. "And any Swiss child with ambition goes to private school. I was national fencing champion for eight years. Won gold twice at the

Olympics."

Her eyes never wavered from the road, yet there existed something colder in her voice now.

Stone raised his eyebrows. "Impressive. And now? Mid-level at your family's bank, bored out of your mind, indulging in reckless driving to fill that empty adrenaline void?"

Cindy let out a sharp, derisive laugh, muttering something under her breath—a mixture of Swiss curses and unflattering comments about Stone's mother. He caught the gist and smiled to himself. *Touché, spoiled brat.*

As they neared the outskirts of Bern, Cindy eased off the accelerator. The wealthier the city, the increased public transport cameras lurked around every corner. Bern, with its status as a financial hub, was under constant surveillance. The watchers were always watching.

Cindy pulled up to a corner near a tram stop, the car idling as she reached down to unlock the doors. She pressed a button to unlock the trunk and turned toward Stone.

"Mr. Stone—if that's even your real name—I don't care what you think of me. My father runs the FIS—Federal Intelligence Service—and if I ever hear of you near my grandmother's inn again, I'll make sure he knows." She leaned closer, her voice dripping with menace. "And trust me, you don't want that."

Before Stone could respond, she reached into her purse and pulled out her phone, raising it in front of his face like a weapon. Stone's reflexes were faster—he snatched it from her hand before she snapped a photo, stepped from the car, and without a second thought, smashed the phone against the pavement.

The shattering sound echoed in the quiet street. Cindy froze for a second, staring at the broken pieces of glass and plastic scattered across the sidewalk. Her fury was palpable.

Stone calmly grabbed his duffel bag from the trunk, slammed it shut, and gave her a mock salute through the rear window. Without looking back, he blended into the flow of pedestrians, vanishing into the crowd. He had a knack for disappearing. how to slip through the cracks without a trace.

Cindy sat there, stunned, her hands gripping the steering wheel. After a moment, she cursed under her breath, putting the car in park as she retrieved her shattered phone. Her pulse quickened with rage. She didn't care what her grandmother said anymore—she intended to reveal everything to her father.

As she sped off, the fury in her chest only grew. She underestimated him, but that would be the final time. Stone wasn't just another drifter. And now, he was a problem she couldn't ignore. Contacting her father will be unpleasant and insightful after learning the real identity of her passenger.

CHAPTER 13

SFPO, Bern

Stone drifted through the bustling crowd, blending in effortlessly as he navigated the streets of Bern. The air thick with aromatic fresh bread and coffee from the corner cafés, the murmur of conversations masking the low whir of the city's CVT cameras. He stayed in the periphery, careful to avoid those watchful eyes, always aware of the invisible net around him. His destination: SFPO, or as the trade called it, Special Forces Personal Office Perks. Located on Münzgraben Boulevard, its entrance being as inconspicuous as its reputation—just a plain door with a number "7," no nameplate, no bell, nothing to suggest the high-stakes world behind it.

SFPO was a lifeline for operatives like Stone. A place where agents quietly stock up on firearms, untraceable cash, safe house keys, and transportation—everything needed to disappear or strike with precision. Stone had been out of the game for some time, and he wondered if they'd still welcome him, or if they'd see him as a relic of a bygone era.

His bruises from the past 24 hours were starting to ache again, the deep purples blooming under his skin. First things first, he needed some gel for the pain. He made his way along the Aare, the river winding through Bern like a shimmering artery, like the Seine in Paris. A useful marker, not only for navigation but for checking if he had a tail. The water rippled in the early evening light, casting a shimmering reflection off the centuries-old stone bridges. Stone veered off the river and slipped into a DROPA, a 24-hour pharmacy, blending into the mundane task of the locals as he grabbed some medical supplies.

SFPO

Stone circled the block around SFPO, taking his time as he moved through narrow alleys and back streets. He scoped the building from every possible vantage point, counting the cameras, gauging the foot traffic. He sensed they were watching him too, just as he'd intended. This wasn't a stealth operation. He wanted them to see him coming, to signal his presence; alone and unarmed. —at least visibly. His duffel bag worn and scuffed from years of use, and adding to his appearance as someone who'd seen better days.

After about thirty minutes of observation, Stone walked directly to the door and pressed the tiny, almost invisible bell. He looked straight into the camera mounted high in the corner, its lens reflecting a tiny glint of sunlight. Seconds stretched into what felt like minutes before the buzz of the door lock echoed in the still street. The entrance clicked open, and Stone moved into the small entryway, at once aware of the reinforced bulletproof glass encasing him.

Two guards stood at attention, their weapons trained on him, silent and icy. These weren't just any guards—they were former special ops, the kind who could read a heartbeat and sense danger before it surfaced. Stone dropped his duffel bag and nudged it away with his foot, moving slowly as he reached into his jacket.

Easy, boys, he thought. The tension in the air was almost palpable to him.

He pulled out his passport and slid it through the narrow envelope slot. One of the guards took it without a word, feeding it into a scanner, his eyes never leaving Stone's. The scanner blinked green, and the guard slid the passport back, dropping it into a bin without a second glance. Being a disposable one anyway—Stone knew he wouldn't get it back.

A second door slid open, and Stone advanced into a new chamber. A sudden blast of air sprayed him from all directions, the chemical scent harsh and sterile, like the disinfectant used in hospital corridors. He held his breath, the smell dragging memories of hospital beds and the dying back into his mind. He hated it.

After what felt like a full minute, the door opened, revealing a young man—just in his twenties, with messy hair and mismatched clothes. He didn't fit in with the militaristic order of the guards.

"Uh, Dr. Stone?" a meekly childlike man asked, his voice uncertain, as if asking a question.

Stone grunted in response, tossing his bag onto the table for inspection. The young man hardly noticed, already walking down the hall as Stone followed. The guards took over the search.

"We, uh, heard about the train incident," the man stated, glancing at Stone before pressing the elevator button. "Lot of chatter across the networks. Debrief and all that coming up, right?"

"I wasn't working," Stone replied, his voice low. He didn't

look up, focusing instead on the sensation of the elevator descending, even though being smoother than most. He could feel it, the subtle pull downward.

The man said nothing, letting the silence hang as the elevator doors opened, revealing a cooler, almost clinical atmosphere below ground. Stone took in the artificial air, the sterile lighting, and followed the kid down the lengthy corridor. He counted each step. Sixty, right turn. He stored it away for later.

The man knocked on a door and entered ahead of him, revealing an older man seated at a plain desk. His grizzled face buried in paperwork; his reading glasses perched on the edge of his nose. Without looking up, he dismissed the kid with a grunt.

"Sit your ass down, Stone. I'm not gonna crane my neck to look at you."

Stone slouched into the chair, resisting the urge to kick his feet up on the desk. The old man's gruff exterior hid a familiar quality, a worn-out routine between them.

"You're a real piece of work, you know that?" the man barked, tossing his pen onto the desk and crossing his arms. The room fell into silence, punctuated only by the soft buzz of the AC and distant footsteps from the hallway.

The old man got up, grabbed two bottles of water from a mini fridge, and tossed one toward Stone without looking. Stone caught it without effort, cracked it open, and took a long drink.

"You're aware the Germans are pissed, right? They canceled a party on the Rhine because of you," the older man remarked, pointing an accusing finger. "Half their agents you've tangled with are out of commission, and they're demanding you be dealt with."

"They're overreacting. The party's overrated anyway," Stone muttered. "Half the women on that boat aren't even women."

The old man roared with laughter, slapping his knees. "Goddamn, Stone, that annual meet and greet always gave us better intel. The annual meet-and-greet was always a treasure trove of Intel," Weisberg grunted, his voice teeming with nostalgia. "Better than any official briefing. Office gossip, loose lips, booze flowing—worth the two-hour boat ride with piss-poor wine and even worse food." He leaned back in his chair, the leather creaking under his weight. "But you, Stone... you stirred the pot. Put five German agents out of commission for six months—three of them they were grooming at a gym in Berlin, and the two on that train." Weisberg's eyes darkened, his tone shifting. "Now the Germans want blood, and they're not picky about whose."

Stone remained still, taking it all in, his senses sharp. The air thick with stale coffee and cigarette smoke, remnants of the old man's extended hours in this office. He could still feel the frigid, clinical air from the underground corridor lingering on his skin. The fluorescent lights hummed faintly, casting a harsh, sterile glow over the room. Stone sipped his water, his mind ticking over the facts as Weisberg spoke. He wasn't in the clear—not by a long shot.

"The head of internal police in Berlin... he's been on my ass for weeks," Weisberg continued, waving a hand in frustration. "Calls every day, ranting about you, Stone. Wanting to handle it themselves. Like they'd have a shot." He gave a dismissive snort. "I told him, 'That's a really bad idea.' Can you imagine those clowns trying to deal with you? The body count they've got on record is laughable compared to the real numbers."

Stone gave a slight smile, but stayed quiet, keeping his thoughts under lock. If he'd truly been in deep, the room likely would be swarming with poorly dressed suits and more firepower than a high school graduation hall. He knew how this game worked—this was just another play. He took an extra sip of water, waiting.

Stone eyes flickered over him. "You look thinner," he said with a raised eyebrow. "Dieting again?"

Weisberg's mouth curled into a smirk. "I look good, don't I?"

Weisberg's face split into a broad grin. "Hell, yeah. That's how I sneak up on the enemy. They see a guy like me and think, 'No way this old sack of shit is dangerous." He winked, tapping his gut. "But when I was your age, I did the work of ten field agents, easy. It's not about muscles, kid—it's about knowing the right people, shaking the correct hands." Weisberg paused, his tone softening. He gave Stone a long, fatherly look. "So, when are you gonna settle down? Find yourself a nice Jewish girl, have some kids?"

Stone let the moment hang in the air. "You know the answer to that. Family's not in the cards for guys like me. You settle down, you end up behind a desk—if you're lucky. Besides, I'm not exactly 'employed' these days." He leaned back in his chair, his tone shifting. "Independent contractor. Disposable. Isn't that how you trained me?"

Weisberg's grin faded, replaced with a look of concern. He leaned forward, his forearms pressing into the desk, muscles still defined from his wrestling days. "Listen, son. You're burned in

Germany. That's not changing. Sure, we'll still play nice with them, but this went all the way up the chain. The President got wind of it—he's not happy."

Stone raised an eyebrow. "The President of the United States knows about me?"

Weisberg chuckled, shaking his head. "Don't flatter yourself, smartass. He knows about the incident, not you. But they offered you a way out—your medical license reinstated overseas. You could go back to practicing, listening to people complain about their bad backs or whatever. It's safe."

Stone stared down at the water bottle in his hands, his fingers tapping the plastic rhythmically. "Not really my thing anymore. I like the contracts that come my way—clean, simple. I don't sleep with one eye open."

Weisberg laughed, a deep, throaty sound. "Bullshit! You've never slept in your life, Stone. And those so-called 'soft' contracts? They were anything but. You think we don't keep tabs on our people? Especially the talented ones like you?"

Stone shrugged, unbothered. "Being a medical support team member in the hot zone wasn't for me. Too... confining. And we both know how the interrogation team felt about me."

Weisberg's grin widened. "Oh, I remember. The sole doctor within the agency's history to inject Propel into the interrogator instead of the detainee." He laughed so hard; he had to wipe his eyes. "Still not sure what really happened that day. I've heard a dozen versions of the story, none of 'em adding up."

Stone said nothing, letting the silence stretch between them, the mystery left unresolved.

CHAPTER 14

The Weasel

Weisberg began to speak, his voice gravelly, when the door flew open, slamming against the wall with a bang that echoed through the room. In sauntered Willy Rice—known to most as "The Weasel." He was a pale, sickly-looking man, his gaunt face and sallow skin giving the impression of someone who seen too much bad coffee and not enough daylight. He'd been a bureaucratic lifer, clinging to his position as head of Europe's special branch long after he should've retired, probably two Desert Storms ago. Despite his unimpressive career in records back stateside, Rice had a knack for weaving tall tales about imaginary behind-the-lines escapades. Around the office, he fancied himself "Wild Bill," though no one took his war stories seriously.

"Weisberg," Rice rasped, his voice like sandpaper as he coughed and cleared his throat, casting a disdainful glance at Stone. His gaze flicked to Stone's intense green eyes before settling on a spot above Stone's head, unwilling to meet his stare directly. "You really fucked things up this time. We should call the boys upstairs, hog-tie you, and deliver you to the Germans ourselves—leave you on the embassy steps and wash our hands of you."

Stone was out of his seat before Rice's brain had even

registered the motion—a blur of controlled fury. He crossed the room in a flash, moving faster than Rice could react. The weasel-like man stumbled back, his eyes wide with fear as he lost his balance. Stone's hand shot out, grabbing him between the neck and shoulder with a grip like iron. Rice's breath hitched, his body jerking upward as Stone effortlessly lifted him onto his toes, squeezing just enough to make a point.

"Stone!" Weisberg barked, his voice cutting through the tension.

Stone held the Weasel's gaze, his own eyes blazing with cold fury. For a moment, the room was silent, except for the shallow, panicked breaths coming from Rice. Stone waited, daring him to speak again.

Weisberg sighed, leaning back in his chair, by all means amused but trying to defuse the situation. "He's not wrong. You did make a hell of a mess, and most of its landing in his lap to clean up. Don't kill the single guy who knows where all the best German hideouts are—here and abroad."

Stone released Rice, letting him stumble back, his knees weak beneath him. The weasel's face flushed, his breathing ragged as he scrambled to regain his composure. Stone casually returned to his seat, his expression unreadable, but his presence still charged with menace.

Weisberg's tone turned crisp as he waved a dismissive hand toward Rice. "Get out, Rice. And don't ever threaten a real war hero again."

The door closed behind Rice, and as soon as he was gone, both men burst into laughter.

"I swear, I think he shat himself!" Weisberg bellowed, his booming laugh filling the room.

Stone shook his head, still smirking. "He's a prick. Always has been. How anyone works with him is beyond me."

"Oh, his bark is worse than his bite," Weisberg wheezed, wiping a tear from his eye. "As you can see."

The laughter subsided, leaving a comfortable silence between the two men. Weisberg leaned back in his chair, his gaze drifting toward the ceiling. "I'm getting too old for this shit." He stretched his arms wide with a yawn, the leather of his chair creaking as he stood up. Without warning, he lumbered over to Stone and enveloped him in a bear hug, the grip was so strong it almost lifted him.

"Let's go get something to eat. And try not to kill anyone on the way out," chuckling again.

Stone noticed the warmth of the embrace but remained on high alert, his mind still calculating as they made their way toward the entrance. Neither man spoke in the elevator, machinery's thrum was the sole sound as they descended toward the main floor. As they proceeded out into the building's lobby, Stone couldn't resist a final parting shot. He looked up at the security camera in the corner of the elevator, mouthed fuck you, and smiled.

Back on the street, the cool air of the city hit them like a wave. It carried the odor of wet pavement and car exhaust, mixing with the faint, sweet aroma of bread baking from a nearby café. Weisberg turned to Stone with a grin, waving cheerfully toward a third-floor window in the apartment across the street. "Smile for the assholes upstairs," he muttered. "Swiss State Security. They've had eyes on us 24/7 since 2011. Bureaucracy at its finest. They say they're 'protecting US personnel,' but we all know what they're in fact doing. Spying on their own damn allies." Weisberg shook his head, chuckling. "They think watching us will lead them to the bad guys. What they should be doing is sending us boxes of Swiss chocolate." His laughter echoed down the street, loud and infectious, but Stone only offered a half-smile, his eyes constantly scanning for threats.

They walked a couple of blocks north, the city bustling with the familiar rhythm of people rushing to and from work. The sounds of distant traffic and murmured conversations filled the air, punctuated by the occasional blare of a horn. Stone's senses remain on high alert, taking in every detail—the flicker of movement in a shadowed alley, the hum of electricity from a streetlamp, the feeling of eyes on them that weren't the Swiss.

They came across a bright yellow storefront, the bold red sign above the door simply read Eat. An American-style diner, out of place but somehow comforting in this foreign city.

Weisberg clapped Stone on the shoulder. "Let's grab a bite. I'm starving, and you look like you could use a proper meal. And don't worry—no Swiss spies in here. Just bad coffee and greasy burgers. My kind of place." Weisberg smiled. Stone just shook his head and opened the door for the older man.

CHAPTER 15

The American style Dinner, Bern

Inside the diner, the air smelled of grease and faint cleaning solution, the kind of nondescript place that no one would ever look twice at. Stone scanned the room automatically—five booths, eight tables. A reflex he couldn't shake, even here in a setting that seemed deliberately unremarkable. They chose the rearmost booth by the kitchen, the one with Stone's back to the entrance, just as he expected. Weisberg slid in across from him with a knowing grin.

"Relax," Weisberg said, with a gruff voice but friendly. "You're among friends. Stop looking over your shoulder for a change."

Stone gave a slight shrug, pretending to consider it, before glancing at the menu in his hands, though his mind still focused on the exits, the corners, and the unfamiliar faces.

His reply was cut short by an overweight, middle-aged woman with dark eyes and hair approached, her worn blue dress fitting the diner's plain aesthetic. Her demeanor, however, was anything but ordinary. She bent down, kissing Weisberg on the cheek, her hand resting on his broad shoulder as though they shared an unspoken connection. Her eyes sparkled with warmth as she extended her hand toward Stone.

"And who's this?" Her voice had a soft rasp, the kind that

spoke of years of hard living.

Weisberg's eyebrows shot up, the flush in his cheeks betraying his usual tough exterior. "Estee, this is—"

"I know who this is," she cut him off, eyes now focused entirely on Stone. "The doctor. He never stops talking about you. Doctor this, doctor that. It's wonderful to finally meet you." She smiled; her expression tinged with admiration. "And handsome too."

Stone took her hand carefully, noting the scar tissue that ran up her wrist to her elbow. Old, but the mark of something that had been painful once. "Estee," she introduced herself with warmth.

"R," Stone replied, looking back at Weisberg. The glance was brief but spoke volumes. Weisberg, the old man who lost his wife more than a decade ago, had after a lengthy time found someone to fill the void. No more needed to be said.

"You boys want the usual?" she asked Weisberg, who grinned, then looked at Stone. "And for the doctor? Some fish, perhaps?"

Stone shook his head. "I'll have what he's having," placing the menu aside. "And an unsweetened iced tea, please."

Estee gave Weisberg's shoulder a gentle pat before walking away. Stone leaned back in the booth, studying his companion. "So."

Weisberg raised his hands defensively, a grin splitting his face. "What can I say? I'm a lady killer," he boomed, his laughter filling the small diner. It was infectious, loud, and somehow managed to chase away the ever-present sense of danger in Stone's mind. But Stone knew better—Weisberg's laughter was genuine, but if you remain on his bad side, your days are numbered.

The moment was interrupted when Estee returned with two towering cheeseburgers and a mountain of fries. The plates clattered onto the table with a satisfying weight.

"Grass-fed beef from the States," Estee said proudly, watching them like a mother who just served up her best dish. "I'll leave you boys to it. Gotta get started on tonight's meatloaf."

Stone bit into the burger, and for a second, all the tension melted away. The beef was juicy, perfectly cooked, the bun soft and fresh. A mere simple pleasure in a life of constant vigilance. He couldn't help but sigh. It was heaven.

They ate in silence; all that could be heard was plates scraping and the occasional satisfied grunt from Weisberg. After polishing off their burgers, Weisberg leaned back, wiping his mouth and grinning.

"So," Weisberg began, his tone shifting to something more serious. "I have a project for you. Perfect for keeping you off the radar while things settle down."

Stone stiffened, glancing up at the picture on the wall behind Weisberg's head. He wasn't looking at the picture—just using it to check the reflections in the glass, watching the entrances and exits. His instincts remained razor-sharp. "I don't like the sound of this," he muttered.

Weisberg raised an eyebrow, his tone calm but firm. "Look, the Germans aren't going to let this go. You know how they are.

They'll hunt you down, and we both know how that ends." He leaned in, his voice dropping. "I'm offering you something to keep you out of sight, off the radar, while I smooth things over with the State Department."

There being no immediate response from Stone. his eyes still fixed on the reflections behind Weisberg.

"Where?" he asked, though his voice betrayed no eagerness. Persuading him wasn't a simple task, even by someone he trusted.

Weisberg smiled, sensing the unspoken agreement. "Nice and warm. You'll love it. Medical officer for a security checkpoint team at an airport. Real simple stuff—no mess, no drama. The team just needs someone to watch over a package."

"And?" Stone's voice is cold, skeptical.

"And what?" Weisberg grinned again. "No hidden agenda. The package has a medical condition, some low blood sugar thing. The team asked for a medical contractor. That's it. You'll be out in the morning."

Stone didn't buy it, but he wasn't about to argue. This wasn't his first "simple job" that turned out to be anything but. Before he could press further, Estee returned, her motherly smile making the conversation feel miles away.

"So, how'd you like the burgers, boys?"

They exchanged pleasantries for another half-hour, arguing over the bill and joking with Estee. The serious tone from earlier faded, replaced by a sense of camaraderie, though it didn't fool Stone. As they left, Weisberg dropped a crisp 100 Euro bill on the table, giving Estee's staff a jovial farewell.

But in the back of Stone's mind, the mission, the Germans, and the unknown variables swirled. Something told him this "soft project" was about to become considerably more complicated.

CHAPTER 16

River Walk

As Stone and Weisberg strolled along the river, the afternoon air hung heavy with the smell of water and distant flowers, a sharp contrast to the tension that always simmered between them. The river's faint rhythmic murmur did little to soothe the weight of the conversation. Stone's limp grew pronounced after a mile, each step biting into him as they discussed the mission.

"The person of interest," Weisberg began, his voice low, "was caught with an ancient artifact. Museum quality. Most likely taken from a historical site. World authorities agreed years ago that the French would hold onto such treasures until their authenticity and origins could be determined." He paused, glancing sideways at Stone. "Of course, people forget Napoleon's penchant for theft, but the French have a short memory for their own crimes."

Stone's expression remained unreadable, but the slight clench of his jaw revealed his irritation. His leg was protesting every step, and he had no patience for the French or their selective memories.

"Let's sit," Weisberg suggested, motioning to a nearby bench. "You're not as young as you used to be, and frankly, I'm in better shape." He chuckled, patting his substantial gut before turning his gaze to Stone's eyes. The moment held a mix of humor and empathy, though both men had long since learned to bury their emotions beneath layers of stoicism.

"It will always be painful, you know," Weisberg said, his voice softening. "Love's that way."

"Really?" Stone replied dryly. "I was thinking more about the pain in my ass, not the person who caused it."

Weisberg raised his hands in mock surrender, a sigh escaping his lips. "Touché." The older man leaned back, his gaze drifting toward the slow-moving river. "Warmer weather will help your joints, trust me. When I travel to the south of Spain, it's like a miracle. Only thing that bothers me is the history. The Jews suffered there, just like everywhere else."

"Every nation has its scars," Stone spoke, in a distant voice, his eyes fixed on the horizon. "Old wounds, new wounds— anti-Semitism's never left. History's just a mirror."

Weisberg nodded, but his expression was weary. Stone could see the weight of his past in the lines on the older man's face. Weisberg a hero, even if he didn't wear it on his sleeve. The number of attacks he'd thwarted on European soil should've earned him every medal there was, but instead, he'd been relegated to this—sorting through the detritus of the past, playing a glorified customs agent for artifacts and relics.

"I know what you're thinking," In a low voice, Weisberg stated, pulling himself from his reverie. "Don't worry about me. I'm content with the pace of things now." He handed Stone a tiny jump drive, his fingers brushing against Stone's for a moment, a rare touch of camaraderie. "Here are the details. Money's being loaded onto your debit card. The staff girls will send you your flight information."

Stone raised an eyebrow. "Girls?"

Weisberg waved a hand dismissively. "What? They're young. They run circles around us with computers these days. Last week, they dropped a Hellfire missile on a terrorist base without batting an eye and then went on about some new nightclub she had to check out."

Stone smirked. "Soon enough, there'll be no place for us dinosaurs."

"There'll always be dirty work, my friend," Weisberg replied, his voice tinged with a sadness that only men who've seen too much understand. "Up close and personal. That's the true way the world functions. "

They continued their walk in silence, their footsteps blending with the distant murmur city. When they reached the edge of the river, Stone turned to leave. "I'll try not to cause any trouble," he said, offering a rare, wry smile.

Weisberg watched as Stone slipped into the crowd, disappeared completely, leaving no sign he was ever present. He marveled at how effortlessly the man could vanish, a ghost in broad daylight. Stone was born for the shadows, a man who couldn't be trained—only unleashed when needed. A dangerous asset, and a friend with an untamable spirit.

Back at his temporary lodging, Stone found a duffel bag waiting for him. Inside was a passport, two credit cards, a debit card, and 2,000 Euros. Tucked inside the passport, a small burner phone and a scrap of paper with a ten-digit passcode. Stone memorized the code, then tore the paper into small pieces, scattering them into the waste bin before leaving the room.

His destination: Bern Airport, a few kilometers away. The Lyft driver, a younger man with an impressive array of piercings, turned in his seat to greet Stone with a halfhearted smile. Stone noticed the infected crust around the driver's piercings, an observation that made him think about his own advancing years. He wondered about his own sustainability. How many more missions before his body would give out?

As they drove through the quiet streets, Stone leaned his head against the window, his mind on the mission ahead. The artifact. The Germans. The soft job that was never just "soft." Subconsciously, he was aware, this was just the calm before the storm. And storms, in his line of work, were never far off.

CHAPTER 17

King Khaled International Airport

At Bern Airport, time crawled. Stone's eyes scanned the brief Weisberg handed over—its cold, clinical details about a man both the U.S. and Israel had long marked as a trafficker. His target, a ghost in the underworld of artifact smuggling and covert transport of wet-work operatives between Palestine and Lebanon, resurfaced. For years, he slipped through the cracks, extracting priceless relics from war-torn Middle Eastern sites. Now, he was caught—but something about it felt too easy.

Stone passed through airport security with his forged credentials without breaking stride, his movements precise, unhurried. He found a simple meal, a bowl of fruit and a sandwich, and positioned himself near the boarding gate for his flight to Riyadh. This wasn't the part of the job that raised his pulse. Patience, discipline—This is what sets professionals apart from everyone else.

The flight being uneventful, though Stone remained on edge. He slept lightly, avoiding the prawn biryani that could spell a bad night at 35,000 feet, and stuck to a salad. As the plane touched down at King Khaled International Airport, the unmistakable heat hit him like a hammer when he stepped outside.

The man approached from the left—sloppy, too direct for Stone's taste. He could smell the man's cologne before he saw him. Stone didn't move, not yet. He let the man grab the handle of his bag, allowing him to step into Stone's range. In one swift motion, Stone pivoted, his iron grip locking on the man's wrist like a vice, his eyes cutting into the Saudi's soul.

The man stammered, his mouth hanging open. Stone didn't need to speak—his silence was enough. The Saudi stood frozen as Stone, ever the professional, released his wrist and moved past him, stepping into the waiting SUV without a word. The man scrambled in behind him.

"Good day, mate," the driver greeted in a feigned Australian accent, honking impatiently as he navigated into a lane. His manner was casual, too casual. Stone filed it away.

They weaved through the streets of Riyadh, taking circuitous routes, detouring into alleyways. The driver's accent grated on Stone, but he played along, keeping his focus outward. He wasn't here for chit-chat. This was work.

The SUV pulled into an office complex, a nondescript security guard manning the gate, unarmed and uninterested. The driver blew him a kiss, mockingly, and sped into the underground garage. Stone already scanning the area, noting entrances and exits. In this profession, the smallest details can mean the difference between life or death.

"This way, mate," the driver chirped, leading Stone inside, not waiting for a response.

Inside the building, Stone sized up his new "guide." Soft around the middle, bloated, and masked behind sunglasses—middle-aged contractors who still fancied themselves operatives, but their best days linger behind them. The man tried to engage in trivial talk, fishing for information. Stone gave him nothing, offering "Mate works," as they exited the elevator and entered a plush reception area, far removed from the chaotic world outside.

Fake Aussie swiped a keycard at a stairwell. "You're here to check a pulse, then we can ship out our guest."

Stone tossed his bag aside carelessly as they entered a room littered with duffle bags, a deliberately chaotic setup.

"I want to see the video of the package at the airport," Stone demanded, his voice flat but firm. No room for negotiation.

Fake Aussie hesitated, then shrugged, mumbling to himself as he booted up a computer. Surveillance footage flickered on the screen—mundane, uneventful for anyone not trained to see the subtleties. The suspect, dragging a carry-on, blended into the crowd. The passport was American, but the rest of him screamed fake—cheap shoes, off-brand clothes.

Stone watched the people around the mule. He spotted them quickly—three Middle Eastern men and one woman. They turned their backs as the local police took down the mule. But what caught his eye was the man in the upper corner of the frame, dressed sharply in western clothes, with a smile that chilled Stone's blood.

He knew that face. Stone zoomed in. His breath caught— just for a moment. He needed to talk to the mule, but this wasn't about the mule anymore.

He snapped a picture of the screen with his mobile phone and encrypted it before sending it off to a dummy account. Weisberg's team being responsible for the remaining tasks. Stone could feel the old instincts kicking in, the ones honed by years of dirty work in the shadows. This wasn't over—not by a long shot.

"You got a med kit here?" Stone asked, his voice calm but purposeful.

Fake Aussie chuckled. "Hell, we've got an operating table, Doc. You want to saw off a limb?"

Stone followed him into a sterile medical room, eyeing the wall-to-wall supplies. He had no intention of performing surgery, but he pocketed the Propofol, paracetamol, and ibuprofen anyway. His leg was throbbing again, the old injury flaring up. He picked up a wooden cane from the locker—it wasn't ideal, but it would do. Pain came with the job, but it didn't have to be unbearable.

"Hey, Doc, I was only kidding about the surgery part," Fake Aussie said with a laugh.

Stone just smiled and gestured for him to lead the way. His leg, now supported by the cane, felt a little better.

CHAPTER 18

The Interrogation

Shadows filled the room, cool and uninviting, yet drenched in sweat from the man chained to the chair. The wooden seat was small, almost mocking in its childlike design, But the man wasn't in any state to laugh. His body strained awkwardly, right arm twisted painfully behind his back, the plastic restraints biting into his wrist. His shoulder blade jutted out unnaturally, teetering on the edge of dislocation. The left arm being no better stretched forward, shackled to the leg of a table bolted to the floor. Every minute movement sent shocks of pain rippling through his spine, his muscles spasming in protest.

His labored breaths were the sole interruption of the room's silence,

the hiss of his discomfort growing with each passing minute. His sweat stung his eyes, turning the dim lighting into a blurry haze, yet, the circumstances were perfectly transparent. Hope couldn't be found here. Rather a place for fear.

In the observation room behind the one-way glass, the team gathered, their eyes locked on the spectacle before them. Every twitch, every grimace, every bead of sweat was a data point to exploit. The man wasn't talking yet, but they accepted that it would happen eventually.

The position they placed him in was designed to maximize

discomfort while keeping the mind alert, teetering on the edge of breaking down. They couldn't leave him in it for too long, though. The body had its limits and eventually gave out and once that happened, getting answers would be harder.

The door behind them opened. "Fake Aussie" and Stone entered. The men gave only a cursory glance upwards, eyes still on the prisoner. Stone's sharp gaze scanned the room, noting the men, the setup, and at last, the object on the table. A partially open package, Hebrew scrawled along its side. His knowledge of the language was a tad rusty—memories of long-abandoned Hebrew school flashed through his mind—but that didn't matter right now.

"Here's the Doc," Aussie grunted, nodding towards Stone, before nonchalantly leaning against the wall, appearing apathetic.

The team leader gave him little attention, focused on the task at hand. "No need for you here, Doc," dismissively. "Subject's close. We've got two hours before transport."

Stone didn't respond. Instead, he tossed a letter onto the table. The team leader frowned, recognizing its significance without needing to read it. Being the authorization Stone needed—control over the interrogation, the subject, and, if necessary, the chemical methods to extract whatever information needed.

A second man in the group leaned closer, smirking at the glass. "He's close. Should we go hard first, soften him up later?"

The rest nodded their heads. Intimidation being their usual tactic—hulking men with grim faces would make most subjects crumble. But sometimes, that only led to babbling—extensive hours of incoherent rambling that would have to be sifted through, piece by piece. Today, they were pressed for time. They needed answers fast, and the main office wasn't going to tolerate any screw-ups.

Stone, silent until now, pushed himself off the wall with his cane. "I'll do it."

The room froze. Stone had broad shoulders, and his movements deliberate and slow. He walked with a hitch, leaning heavily on his cane, there was an intensity about him. Something dangerous.

The muscular man who suggested the hard approach sneered. "Guess we're going with the kid gloves method, then."

Stone paused mid-stride, glancing back just enough to reveal a faint, almost imperceptible smile. Just the team leader caught it.

"That's enough!" the team leader barked, silencing the room. "Watch and learn."

As Stone made his way to the door, a newer team member muttered under his breath. "Who is this guy?"

"Freelance," the team leader replied, his voice low and frosty.

"Not another spook," the muscular man grumbled.

The team leader's gaze turned icy. "I didn't say that. He's worse than a ghost. No ties, no strings. And once we're done, we pretend he was never here."

Silence followed as Stone slipped into the interrogation room. The team watched through the glass, their attention now divided between the prisoner and Stone.

At the center of the room, the artifact sat ominously on the table—a two-foot cylinder, its seal partially torn open by an overzealous customs agent. The agent hadn't realized the significance of the object, or how his impatience sealed his fate. The man found dead with an anchor chain around his neck, washed up on the shores of Key West. The package he'd tampered with was an important archaeological find in decades, and now it sat here, in the middle of an interrogation chamber, while a man slowly broke.

Trafficking cultural treasures had become big business, funding everything from terrorist organizations to private collectors with more money than morals. Ancient coins, fossilized relics, artifacts— with the right connections, anything can be smuggled. But now, they possessed something bigger, something dangerous.

Stone stood before the prisoner; his expression unreadable. The prisoner's breathing hitched as their eyes met. The team paid close attention, knowing that what happened next could decide the fate of more than just the man in the chair.

Stone didn't need brute force. He had something far more effective- time and patience.

CHAPTER 19

Switching Sides

As Stone entered the corridor, a weight seemed to lift from his shoulders. The testosterone-heavy atmosphere behind him, synthetic or otherwise, always worn on him. He couldn't help but wonder when any of those guys last engaged in a real conversation that didn't involve bullets or blood. The hallway was dim, the smell of antiseptic or chemicals sharp in his nostrils, irritating his nose like a persistent itch.

The building had a frigid, dead feel to it, like something forgotten underground. Stone was used to strange environments, but this one felt particularly off—a bomb shelter buried half a mile beneath the surface, one of many scattered across the Kingdom for the royal family. At least a thousand such places existed, their real purpose never fully revealed. It wasn't Stone's job to care, but the thought nagged at him as he advanced through the poorly lit hall, the lone sound the hiss of automatic doors sealing behind him. His steps echoed faintly, absorbed by the thick concrete surrounding him, silencing the world outside.

When he reached the interrogation room marked by a solitary red dot, he paused. The hot seat, they called it, meant to break a man, designed for pain and fear. The faint sense of dread washed over Stone, but he dismissed it. He'd faced tougher circumstances before. He'd faced worse men.

He looked up at the camera above the door, and it opened with a mechanical hiss. As he nudged the door open with his shoulder, he noted the weight of it—sturdy, thick, meant to hold in more than just air. As he entered, a wave of stifling heat hit him. The air was thick and oppressive, like stepping into an oven in the middle of the desert. He glanced at the thermostat: 128 degrees. That explained the sweat pouring off the restrained man. Stone made a quick gesture, slicing his hand across his throat and pointing downward, signaling to lower the temperature and bring in some air.

At first, the man in the chair didn't notice him. He sat facing the opposite direction, his body locked in a twisted position that radiated pain. The restraints were tight, cutting off most of his movement, but the heat had done its real work. He was slick with sweat, trembling as his muscles spasmed under the pressure. When the faint breeze from the cooling fan touched the back of his neck, the man visibly relaxed for a brief moment, imagining a reprieve that wasn't coming. Stone approached silently, unheard by him, nor saw him until stone's hand touched the dislocated shoulder.

The reaction became instant panic. The man bolted upright, or as possible in his compromised state. The pain that shot through him was excruciating, but it was the cold, calculated hand on his shoulder that terrified him. He began to shake uncontrollably, his body betraying him, but Stone stayed silent. His hand remained, a quiet threat, a reminder of who was in control.

Stone leaned in, his voice low and too faint for the room's microphones to pick up. A private conversation now, one just between the two of them. All the interrogation team could do was watch; they remained helpless, as Stone began to work. They were able to observe the subject's reaction, though—the terror in his eyes, the way his body stiffened, the slight dimming of the lights as the man's heart rate spiked dangerously. The team leader studied the monitors. The subject was on the edge, teetering on a precipice that, if crossed, may ruin everything.

Stone moved in front of the subject now, pulling up a chair and sitting across from him. The man's wide eyes met his, and the fear was unmistakable. Stone smiled. With a knowing smile, the kind that said he understood far more than the man hoped he ever would.

The team leader watched the two men with growing unease. Something wasn't right. He underestimated Stone—he thought of him just another hired gun, a freelancer with a reputation but no real ties. But now he wondered if they let something far more dangerous into the room. Not merely fear, but horror consumed the seated man, like he saw a ghost from his past.

"Vitals?" the leader barked, his voice tense.

"He's holding at 165 bpm," the medic responded, eyes glued to the screen. "But he's close to breaking. We've got maybe 20 minutes before he hits the wall." The sensor was attached to the bottom of the integrating table and pointing at the man in the chair.

Inside the room, Stone kept his calm demeanor. He spoke again; his tone gentle but laced with something darker. "Hello, David." The words like a knife, cutting through the subject's mental defenses. Stone had him now. He repeated the name, and the man's breath hitched in his chest. His real name—the name no one was supposed to know.

The leader in the observation room swore under his breath. "How the hell does he know his real name?"

"Should we intervene?" a team member asked nervously.

"No," the leader snapped. "Not yet. Let's see where this goes."

With David restrained, his world began to collapse. He went by a different name for years—Abual—a name that kept him safe, hidden in the shadows of a dangerous life. No one knew his real identity, not even the people closest to him. Yet somehow, this stranger across from him had seen through all of it.

"They would pay handsomely for you, David," Stone said, his voice soft and measured. "The Israelis, the Syrians—hell, half the Middle East will be lining up for a piece of you."

David's heart pounded in his chest, the lights dimming a bit again as the interrogation team monitored his vitals. His mind raced. How is it possible this man knows? A cold sweat broke across his brow as memories he buried deep resurfaced—his mother, a Hebrew woman; his father, a Palestinian, involved in the early days of the PLO.

Stone leaned back, stretching his arms over his head, clearly enjoying the power he wielded. The temperature in the room dropped another few degrees, but David hardly noticed. His mind was in turmoil, struggling to reconcile how his entire life had been exposed in a matter of minutes.

"Where is the second cylinder, David?" Stone's voice cut

through his thoughts like a razor. "You know what I'm talking about. Don't play dumb with me. You've already lost one. You're not going to make it out of here if you don't tell me where the other one is."

David's body convulsed as the pain from his restraints flared up again, but the real pain was in his mind. He was stuck in a game he couldn't win, with nowhere to escape.

"I know who you are," David managed to rasp. His voice, while weak, showed defiance. He glared at Stone, trying to summon some of the strength that had kept him alive all these years. "I know what you did in Lebanon."

Stone smirked, Lebanon's mention as a threat was almost insignificant. He leaned forward, his eyes locking onto David's with a predatory intensity. "Of course you do," his voice dripped with condescension. "But that's not what matters here, David. What matters is whether you tell me what I want to know before they come in here and tear you apart for answers."

David trembled, the words hitting him harder than any physical blow could. He wasn't afraid of death—but the slow, methodical destruction that awaited him in this room? That was a different kind of fear altogether.

"I need you to focus, we don't have much time. They will torture you for information that is meaningless. I, on the other hand, can grant you freedom. How do you think I was able to walk into the room alone?" Stone began to whisper. He switched to Hebrew which he knew the subject understood for he lived in Israel and occupied territories for years before moving overseas to Europe.

"You brought only one cylinder, and you foolishly chose to upgrade to first class. They spotted you a mile away, you fool. Even a halfwit on his first day on the job could pick you out of a crowd."

Stone placed pressure on the cane and stood up to stretch his leg and slowly sat on the desk sideways looking down at the man. He continued in Hebrew "where is the other cylinder? Did you really think you could take it on the open market yourself?"

Stone stood up, placing his hand on the door as if to leave. "Last chance," he said, without turning around. "Where is the second cylinder?"

David's breath came in shallow, panicked bursts. His heart raced. He understood his time was up.

CHAPTER 20

Escape

Stone's instincts kicked in like clockwork. He spun with surgical precision, his left hand striking out in a blur. Two fingers drove into the hollow just below the man's clavicle, a calculated jab targeting both the carotid artery and the cervicobrachial plexus. A move designed to paralyze, not kill—an instant shutdown of the man's motor functions and blood flow to the brain. Stone only just registered the gurgled gasp as the subject slumped, his consciousness snuffed out like a candle in the wind.

But Stone wasn't done. His left leg swept out in a seamless motion, catching the leg of the chair and sending it toppling over. The man's body tumbled, arms still restrained, the harsh angle causing an audible pop as his shoulder dislocated. The crack of his skull hitting the floor followed a second later, the sound muffled but unmistakable. Stone knew the man was out cold. He wouldn't be getting up anytime soon. By the time he woke up, his head throbed like he'd been kicked by a mule, but Stone didn't waste a second worrying about it.

Looking back wasn't necessary for him. His eyes were already on the door.

Beyond the heavy steel, Stone knew the interrogation team was mobilizing. They'd heard the commotion, saw the flicker of motion on the security cameras. Their arrival was imminent.

Stone positioned himself just shy of the door's arc; his posture deceptively relaxed. His feet set shoulder-width apart, knees tent, the cane held loosely in front. He slowed his breathing, lowering his heart rate, focusing. In moments, they'd burst in, guns drawn, running standard hostage-clearance protocol. It would be chaos.

He'd be ready.

The lead bruiser being the first to arrive, definitely the biggest man on the team. A hulking brute, all brawn and little subtlety. He swiped his badge across the lock with a gruff swipe, impatience oozing from his every movement. The rest of the team wasn't even in position yet, their weapons still swinging toward the door. Protocol was slipping—too much bravado, too little caution. The massive man, blind to the risks, thought this would be simple. There were no visible weapons in the room. Each of them had undergone a search, and this guy—this supposed cripple with a cane—was no Houdini.

It would be easy. A walk in the park.

The bruiser let out a bellowing war cry, a guttural sound that echoed down the sterile hallway, the kind of primal scream soldiers were trained to use in basic combat. Meant to strike fear in the hearts of enemies, but in truth, it being more for the attacker—to push past their own fear. Stone knew that sound. He'd heard it before in every conflict zone from Beirut to Kandahar. It meant nothing to him now.

He closed his eyes, his breathing steady, waiting.

The team leader's arrival coincided with the door opening, horror dawning on his face. He watched in dismay as his team rushed the room in a disorganized surge, charging in like cattle squeezing into a crowded elevator, their focus scattered. He could already see the disaster unfolding, the telltale signs of overconfidence and reckless speed.

This was going to end badly.

The massive man came through the door, barreling forward like a battering ram. His focus locked on Stone, the so-called cripple, still standing, still unmoving. He grinned beneath his helmet, already imagining the satisfying crunch of bone as he knocked the man aside.

But Stone had already anticipated his every move.

CHAPTER 21

Dead End

Stone didn't need to open his eyes; the room told him everything. The air shifted as the massive one barreled toward him, reeking of cheap aftershave and overconfidence. His right hand gripped his weapon, but his left arm was outstretched like a linebacker in a clumsy charge. The brute thought he'd crush Stone, and ask questions later. As he closed the distance, he slowed for just a moment, puzzled by Stone's calm demeanor—arms crossed, his cane leaning on his left leg, eyes shut as if oblivious. That fleeting hesitation would be his undoing.

The behemoth raised his left arm, aiming to choke the life out of Stone, but Stone moved first. His eyes shot open just as he sensed the air moving from an approaching hand. In an instant, he shifted his weight, stepping back with his right foot into a classic Seisan-dachi stance, a perfect balance of defense and counterattack. His posture shifted, body angled leaning from the attacker, the cane rising fluidly to meet the brute's forearm. With a subtle twist of the wrist and a calculated pull, Stone used the giant's momentum against him.

In a blink, Stone moved into the brute's charge, their bodies colliding as one, but Stone was already in control. His left leg slid forward, transferring his weight effortlessly to his right, bending his knees as he yanked the cane. The brute never stood a chance—

his enormous frame was hurled over Stone's body, crashing into the far wall. His legs smacked the mirror, and his head collided with the floor with a sickening crack, the unmistakable sound of a skull splitting, like a watermelon dropped from a height.

But Stone wasn't interested in the aftermath. The ex-Marine unconscious—no longer a threat. Stone had already pivoted, his focus shifting to the following group storming the room. As he anticipated, the team spread out upon entering, their formation broken by the massive man now lying unconscious on the floor. With guns drawn, a sense of apprehension hung in the air—unsure how an unarmed man had just dismantled their strongest member. The moment of hesitation was all Stone needed.

In one fluid motion, Stone launched into a somersault, rolling toward the door. The team, trained to clear rooms rather than prevent escapes, reacted too late. Their weapons tracked him, but the first intruder's body blocked their line of fire. Stone's roll carried him out the door and into the hallway. He popped up mid-stride, colliding chest-first with the team leader. Without missing a beat, Stone drove his forehead into the man's face, sending him crumpling to the ground with a shattered nose.

Before the rest could recover, Stone slammed the door shut. The automatic lock clicked into place—now solely operable from the outside. The interrogation team, elite as they were, trapped in their own room, powerless to stop him.

Stone exhaled, scanning the hallway. Darkness. Silence. The path ahead was clear, at least for now. He had to move, and fast. Reinforcements might be coming soon enough, but for the moment, he was alone.

He pressed himself against the wall while moving, one hand trailing against the cool surface for balance, ready to react at a moment's notice. The moans of the team leader behind him faded as Stone proceeded deeper into the facility. The man was probably too preoccupied nursing his shattered nose to pose any threat. Stone had time, but not a lot.

Ahead, he spotted the entrance to the interrogation control room. Empty. Stone slipped inside, his movements swift and purposeful. On the desk, a security badge lay unattended. He snatched it up, pocketing it as his eyes scanned the room. His gaze landed on a small cylinder—a key component in his plan. He wrapped it in a discarded security jacket, tucking it under his arm.

A computer screen flashed with a warning—a large image of Stone's face blaring across the monitor. He chose not to read it. He already knew what it said. Without hesitation, he hit the delete button, erasing the record before slipping back out into the hallway.

His heart rate steady, his mind calm, Stone moved forward. The clock was ticking, and it wouldn't be long before they sent additional men after him. But for now, he was one step ahead— right where he needed to be.

CHAPTER 22

Ride UP

The ride to the surface was swift, but Stone felt each second stretch as the elevator ascended. When the doors slid open, he stepped out into a dim lit corridor, his bag slung over one shoulder. He felt the weight of time pressing against him, each step echoing louder than the preceding. The hallway stretched before him, sterile and silent. Stone's heart was steady, his mind sharper than ever—he didn't have the luxury of panic. The main lobby was ahead, and his escape depended on the succeeding critical moments.

As he approached the lobby, a young officer stood at his post, hand resting on the sidearm holstered at his hip. Stone sized him up in an instant: fresh out of training, inexperienced, and uncertain. Perfect. If push came to shove, there wouldn't be significant resistance.

"Officer," Stone spoke calmly, flashing his badge just enough to catch the light. Neither photos nor names appeared on these badges—security protocol here was deliberately vague. In a facility like this, anonymity was everything. No faces, no names, no questions.

The officer squinted at the badge, his brow furrowing. "Sir?" He hesitated. The man in front of him wasn't in uniform and didn't appear restrained, but something felt off. The computer screen beside him flashed a silent alert: Code 6—security breach. No sirens, no alarms. Just a flashing indicator telling him to stay alert. The young officer's heart raced; he'd been on this post for hours without incident. Now, uncertainty gnawed at him. Fresh out of the academy, stationed here because of his father's pull—a quiet, low-risk assignment. He was supposed to stay out of trouble, just follow orders, but now...now what?

"Stay sharp," Stone said coolly, his voice cutting through the young officer's indecision. "A Code 6's been activated. I'm with the interrogation team."

The officer swallowed hard, glancing at the screen again. He hadn't seen anyone in hours, but now this man, this contractor, was telling him there was a breach? "Y-Yes, sir, but I—"

Stone cut him off with a dismissive wave, stepping past him with a calm authority. "No time for that. Just keep your eyes open."

The officer's mind raced as the larger man disappeared through the gate, stepping into the suffocating heat outside. He should've known more about this place, this situation, but he didn't. Most of the real action happened at night, or so they said. While he bunked in some far-off corner, the heavy hitters were here—doing whatever it was they did in these secretive underground chambers. He only worked as the gatekeeper, told to watch the screen and answer the phone if it rang.

"Sir?" he called out one final time, But Stone had disappeared, stepping into the humid street, leaving the young guard second-guessing himself. When the team leader did manage to recover and get to the control room to release his team, more than an hour had passed since Stone departure and they needed to clear out without the detainee leaving with the door ajar and uncuffed. Heads would roll the team leader knew.

The transition from the cool, sterile facility to the hot, chaotic world above was jarring. The heat hit Stone like a wave, thick and oppressive. He moved fast, scanning the street as he approached the main boulevard a block away. The air smelled of sweat, car exhaust, and desperation—a stark contrast to the controlled environment below. Stone reached into his pocket and pulled out a crisp $50 bill, raising his hand at the curb. The traffic was loud, horns blaring as vehicles jockeyed for position.

Within seconds, a black Chevrolet SUV screeched to a stop before him, the back door popping open. A compact boy leapt out, grinning as he gestured for Stone to climb in. Stone slid into the backseat, and the boy slammed the door behind him, hopping into the front adjacent to his father, his smile wide with excitement. They had won the race to pick up an American—a rare and profitable fare.

As the SUV pulled away from the curb, Stone leaned back and glanced at the driver. "Take me to the airport," in English, his voice steady. "And make it quick."

The driver nodded, his eyes catching Stone's in the rearview mirror. Stone's mind drifted for a moment—he wondered if he'd used a Chinese Yuan instead of an American bill, might the result have been the same? Probably. Money spoke every language.

The streets blurred by as the SUV sped through the city. Stone's thoughts shifted back to the mission. Only a matter of time before the lower-level breach is discovered. The silent Code

6 alert would eventually trigger a full lockdown. It was essential for him to be far away by then, out of reach before anyone could connect the dots.

As the car weaved through traffic, A flicker of unease touched Stone. There remain too many variables. Too many unknowns. But he had come this far, and failure was not an option. The real game was just beginning.

CHAPTER 23

Riyadh Airport

The SUV shot into traffic with a sudden jolt, sideswiping a donkey-pulled vendor cart. The sound of cursing merchants echoed through the half-ajar windows, but the driver's focus was elsewhere. His foot pressed the accelerator harder, speeding up to nearly 70 miles per hour. He glanced nervously in the rearview mirror, eyes shifting between the road ahead and the foreigner sitting in his backseat.

"American?" the driver asked in broken English, tilting his head towards the rearview mirror. The passenger remained motionless, eyes locked ahead, as if completely unaware of the question. His silence unnerved the driver. Most foreigners in this part of the world traveled with security or hired drivers. But this man sat alone, with no luggage, as calm as if he were a tourist on vacation. That left the driver only one conclusion: the man was an assassin.

His hand hovered over the center console, where an old 9mm handgun rested, a relic from a friend who had warned him about the rising crime. His heart pounded, imagination running wild. Was this the end? He could almost feel the cold steel pressed to the back of his head. His grip tightened on the steering wheel, and he glanced nervously at the gun.

He turned somewhat, stealing a look at the man again. The

passenger had a cane resting on his lap, with what appeared to be a uniform jacket draped neatly across it. Was this just an ordinary man with a limp? Or was it all a facade? The driver's mind raced with paranoia.

"I said, are you American? Canadian maybe?" the driver asked again, his voice cracking with forced casualness. Silence. The passenger's refusal to acknowledge him made the situation unbearable. Desperate, the driver muttered a curse under his breath in Arabic. "Your mother is a dog," he spat. The boy in the front seat laughed, enjoying the insult.

As they pulled into the congested lane near the French airline terminal, the driver's patience snapped. He wanted the foreigner out of his car, and fast. Unable to get close to the curb, he barked in Arabic, "Here!" with exaggerated slowness, as if speaking to a child. The boy chuckled again, with a presence of trace of disappointment in his eyes, knowing there'd be no luggage to unload, no extra tip.

The foreigner handed the driver a crisp twenty-dollar bill, which made the driver's eyes flare with anger. Just as he prepared to voice his displeasure, the passenger raised his hand calmly, silencing him.

In flawless Arabic, the man said, "Do you think insulting your customers will bring you wealth?" The driver froze, his hand twitching away from the gun. "And you," the passenger continued, turning to the boy, "find a better driver—one who doesn't run the air conditioning with the windows down. Oil will run out soon, even here."

The driver stiffened as the man strolled out, his demeanor

icy and controlled. With a flick of his wrist, the passenger tossed a rolled-up fifty-dollar bill into the boy's lap. The boy's face lit up with a smile, while the driver cursed, slamming his foot on the accelerator, swerving back into traffic. The boy waved gleefully from the side window as the SUV disappeared into the chaos.

Stone watched them fade into the distance before turning toward the entrance of the terminal. He made sure to look directly into the security camera before stepping inside. The cool air inside was a stark contrast to the oppressive heat outside, but he wasn't here to check in. He proceed deliberately through the terminal, bypassing the main lines and ticket counters, until he reached an unmarked exit door leading to the adjacent building.

Outside, a lone security guard stood near a door marked Maintenance. He noticed Stone approaching, his pace unnervingly steady. This was where passengers typically went for a final cigarette, but this man wasn't stopping. The guard felt an unease creep over him.

"Hello," Stone said, producing a photo ID and a sleek black card. "My driver dropped me at the wrong entrance. Had to walk all the way around."

The guard gave the card a cursory glance then shrugged. His shift was almost over, and his focus was on the chickpea and couscous dinner his wife had prepared for tonight. He wasn't going to hold things up. He unlocked the door, letting Stone inside.

As Stone walked down the dimly lit corridor, his mind sharpened. This was no ordinary terminal. This was where the diplomats and the elite moved unseen, where the stakes were higher, and security tighter. His cane clicked against the floor with each step, a sound barely audible against the hum of distant machinery. By the time he reached the final door, his heart rate hadn't budged, but his instincts were on full alert.

The door clicked open, and he stepped through into a lavishly furnished waiting room. A young woman in a designer suit greeted him with a rehearsed smile. "Good afternoon, sir. May I see your destination papers?"

Stone reached into his pocket, handing over his diplomatic card and driver's license. The irony wasn't lost on him: two flimsy pieces of plastic granting him access to some of the most secure places in the world. The woman's smile grew wider when she saw the card.

"From Chicago?" she asked, her eyes lighting up. "That's my hometown."

"Been a while since I've been back," Stone replied, a casual smile playing on his lips. "Too much travel. And I'm not eager to get caught in another Chicago snowstorm."

They shared a knowing laugh, the kind that comes with mutual understanding of harsh Midwest winters. She gestured for him to sit, offering him a drink while his paperwork was processed.

As she tapped away at her keyboard, the woman couldn't help but glance at him again. There was something about him— older, certainly, but with a quiet power that made her feel both intrigued and cautious. He was no ordinary businessman.

Stone returned the look with a warm smile, his eyes scanning the room, noting every exit, camera, and potential threat.

He had faced tougher situations previously, but this place had its own unique dangers. Even as the woman handed him his boarding pass with a flirtatious smile, he understood this tranquility was fleeting.

The woman hesitated, then asked, "What brings you to Paris?"

He leaned in, his voice low but firm. "Business. But the kind that doesn't always make the headlines."

Her eyes widened a little at his words, but before she asked more, he stood up, tucking the ticket into his coat pocket. "Thanks for your help, Catherine," glancing at her name tag.

For a moment, she was frozen, caught in the magnetic pull of his presence. But Stone had already moved on, his thoughts elsewhere. The moment he stepped onto the plane, he knew the clock was ticking. By the time he landed in Paris, his enemies would be ready.

Thus, the hunt commenced.

CHAPTER 24

Tel Aviv, Israel

The sun crept slowly over the hills of Gilberta, casting a warm, amber glow over Tel Aviv's upscale neighborhood. The quiet streets of the Bauhaus district bathed in the early morning light, a peaceful calm before the city's usual hustle would awaken. Tel Aviv, the largest metropolitan area in Israel, perched proudly on the Mediterranean coast, a mere 60 kilometers northwest of Jerusalem, braced itself for once again sweltering day. Today's forecast predicted a staggering 118 degrees Fahrenheit—record-breaking heat for March, with no relief in sight.

That's why she began her run before dawn.

The runner slipped out of her luxurious townhouse at precisely 5:35 a.m., her long, toned legs carrying her through the Bauhaus district. Her strides were fluid, purposeful, each step a measured beat in the rhythmic pulse of the waking city. She turned down Dizengoff Boulevard, her sneakers tapping lightly on the pavement, and then veered left onto King George Street, heading toward the bustling Carmel Market.

As she passed the local kosher bakery at precisely 6:00 a.m., the middle-aged baker, round and heavyset, caught sight of her. From his stool in the doorway, he gave her a wave and a warm grin. She returned the gesture with a nod, never breaking her pace. Every morning for the past three years, the baker had watched her glide by—a disciplined blur of grace. He admired her punctuality. His wife, amused by his routine admiration, often teased him: "A woman like that would kill you!" They'd both laugh, and she'd shake her head, retreating into the shop while he resumed waiting for the day's first customer.

What the baker didn't know was that his wife's playful comment carried more truth than he realized. The runner, Gabriella Flechtheim, had spent over a decade with the Mossad, Israel's feared intelligence agency, working in a covert division known as "The Club." After fulfilling her mandatory military service, like all Jewish settlers, she had enrolled in medical school in Paris, excelling at the prestigious Pierre and Marie Curie University. Yet, despite her talents in internal medicine, fate pulled her toward archaeology—her true passion.

Now, as a respected professor at Tel Aviv University, Gabriella specialized in ancient artifacts, applying the same keen observation skills she honed in the field with Mossad. Her colleagues and students alike remain in awe of her ability to uncover clues others missed. She had recently participated in part of a groundbreaking archaeological discovery—a hidden tomb beneath Jerusalem. Though her department head had taken credit, her name received only a passing mention in the report, a quiet recognition of her work. She often thought about the injustice during her runs, using the rhythmic pounding of her feet to release her frustrations.

Gabriella increased her pace, the temperature rising with the sun as she advanced along Ramat Yam Boulevard, hugging the coastline. The cool breeze off the Mediterranean offered a brief respite from the oppressive heat. Her morning run was a ritual.

The physical exertion grounded her, a necessary counterbalance to the academic frustrations and the political intrigue that had once defined her life. Her career in archaeology, with its false leads and forgery-laden discoveries, could be maddening. But her runs? Those never disappointed.

As she neared the end of her route, sprinting up Basel Hill Road, Gabriella allowed herself a rare smile. The sweat poured off her body in rivulets, dripping like rain, and she reveled in the feeling. Every muscle burned with satisfaction. This was her escape—a temporary reprieve from the labyrinthine politics of academia and the specters of her past life in espionage.

After she finished, her journey home was not direct. Instead, Gabriella, ever cautious, continued past her flat, walking an extra block before crossing the street to double back. Old habits die hard. Her Mossad training was ingrained deeply, and she instinctively scanned her surroundings, checking for anything or anyone out of place—delivery men lingering too long, strangers walking pets at unusual times. The all-clear given by her internal radar, she returned to her townhouse.

She punched in the twelve-digit code to her security system manually, eschewing the remote opener the system offered. She had been warned by a Mossad technician that those kinds of devices were susceptible to hacking.

Even a teenager with the proper equipment can steal a code from a distance. She entered her cool, shaded hallway and stopped, holding her breath for a full 45 seconds. She listened. Silence. Satisfied, she exhaled and headed to the kitchen, grabbing a pitcher of water from the refrigerator. In Israel, they never wasted water from the tap for drinking. It was a scarce and precious resource.

As she removed her shoes and socks, Gabriella's phone chirped from the living room—a text message. She ignored it for now, opting to begin her post-run stretches instead. It could wait.

After a shower, she picked up her phone and saw the message.

"Call me."

There was no number attached, but Gabriella didn't need one. She recognized the signature encrypted burst—sent via satellite from miles above the earth. The person's identity was clear to her.

A month had passed since she last saw him, at a fundraiser for the new prime minister. She hadn't wanted to go, but he had insisted, enticing her with promises of high-level networking and fine dining. "You could use some fattening up with all that running and crazy exercise," he had joked. She hated that comment, but worse, she hated knowing she was being watched—followed, even. His "unseen companions," as he called them, were never far from her.

Gabriella stepped onto her balcony, scanning the streets below. Despite never seeing them, she sensed their gaze upon her. The General, her old Mossad handler, always kept close. "Guarding angels," he called them. She dialed the number from memory, not bothering to save it in her phone. Too risky.

The phone rang four times before the gravelly voice answered.

"Shalom?"

"Hello, Pappy. Did I wake you?"

Mosesha, the retired general, barked a laugh. "Gabriella, my mamala. It's never too early for you. How's my girl?"

She braced herself. Every conversation with him began this way, but it never ended without a request. A mission. A favor. Something she had promised herself she never get dragged into again.

"I'm retired," she reminded him, her voice harder than she intended.

"Of course, of course," he replied smoothly, the smile evident in his tone. "But there's something you'll find... irresistible. Lunch today. Herzliya Pituach. One o'clock. I'll bring the halibut."

The line went dead before she could argue.

CHAPTER 25

The Beach

Gabriella turned her back on the seaside resort, her gaze locked on the Mediterranean Sea. The sun reflected off the water's surface, creating a dance of light across the diverse shades of green and blue. The view was breathtaking, and she understood why artists and beach lovers were drawn to this secluded cove. A place where the world seemed to pause.

General Moshe watched her from a distance, his eyes never leaving her as she wandered toward the water's edge. The gentle waves lapped at her bare feet as she stood there, her turquoise skirt swaying with the breeze, patterned with vibrant designs he couldn't quite make out. The white, sleeveless blouse she wore clung to her tanned, athletic shoulders, revealing her strength beneath the delicate fabric. Her wrist bore a simple band watch, an understated accessory for someone of her skills.

He smiled as the wind playfully tousled her dark hair, and she brushed it aside without care. There was something childlike in the way she moved, as if the weight of the world had momentarily lifted. But Moshe knew better. Beneath her seemingly carefree demeanor, there was a sharp mind, constantly calculating. She angled herself just so, keeping the sun from blinding her, and as she stretched and twisted her body, it wasn't the casual movements of someone enjoying the sea breeze. She was scanning her surroundings, preparing.

Smart girl, Moshe thought, taking a sip of his iced tea. Very smart.

He glanced at the morning's paper, the Tel Aviv Gazette. Page 8. A seemingly innocuous article about torrential rains in Paris. The Seine was rising, threatening the Louvre, among additional historical sites. Due to an unexplained pressure change, the museum closed for three days. Moshe's lips curled. To the casual reader, it was merely a logistical note, a routine precaution. But Moshe knew this was just the beginning. The Louvre wasn't just closing to protect its treasures from rising water. No, something far more significant was happening, and his team had three days to act.

Gabriella, having taken a final deep breath of the sea air, turned and walked toward the small shack restaurant nearby, her sandals swinging from her hand in a carefree rhythm. As she approached, she scanned the tables. Locals and a couple of tourists scattered around, along with a group of Asian travelers snapping photos of their food and the restaurant's interior. Travel bloggers, she thought with mild amusement, always documenting every mundane detail of their lives.

Her attention was abruptly stolen by booming laughter. "Shalom, mamala!" a deep voice called out. She turned just in time to be enveloped in the iron grip of a large man with a perfectly combed head of gray hair. General Moshe. His laughter echoed across the beach as he lifted her off the ground, planting a kiss on each of her cheeks.

"Enough, enough!" she protested, half-heartedly, "Put me

down before you break something."

Moshe set her down gently, his laughter still rumbling. "You're too light. Even the wind could blow you away! You should put rocks in your pockets, just in case."

She smiled, masking the concern she felt. He looked older and tired than the last time she had seen him. "You're looking well," she quipped, glancing at his distended belly. "Eating for two, I see."

"Someone has to!" he retorted, his laughter booming once more.

As they sat, Moshe's eyes flicked to the Asian tourists at the nearby table. He watched as a waiter 'accidentally' knocked over a pitcher of water onto their cameras. Amidst their protests, the waiter whisked the camera away, promising to dry it off. Moshe knew the memory card wouldn't survive the trip to the kitchen, but the camera would return unharmed. His people were thorough. Everywhere he went, they watched. And in return, he watched the world for them.

After the obligatory pleasantries, Moshe's tone shifted. "What do you think of the Louvre's pressure mishap?"

"What?" Gabriella asked, her brow furrowing. "I haven't heard anything about it."

"Strange. A scholar like you, disconnected from the pulse of such an event?"

"I'm hardly a scholar, Moshe," she replied, using his first name, a sure sign she was annoyed. "Digging up dirt is my preference these days."

Moshe's smile was disarming, but Gabriella wasn't fooled. There was something else behind his calm exterior. "Just come out with it," she sighed, her patience thinning.

Before Moshe responded, the waiter arrived with their meal—freshly grilled halibut, couscous with dates, and a touch of olive oil. Moshe's iced tea was replenished with lime, not lemon, just as he liked. A lemonade was placed in front of Gabriella, complete with a colorful umbrella.

She laughed; the tension momentarily breaking. "You know me too well."

Moshe's gaze softened. "I know what you like. And I know you haven't been eating properly."

As they ate, Moshe spoke in detail about the Louvre. The removal of artifacts, the relocation of priceless works of art. He emphasized the dangers, the high stakes. Fires, floods, accidents. But Gabriella sensed something darker lurking behind his words.

"So now Israel is in the business of stealing artwork on moral grounds?" she asked, her voice edged with skepticism.

"You know how the French are," Moshe replied smoothly. "One minute, we're their saviors. The next, we're a nuisance. But there are pieces in that museum that belong to Jewish families, pieces that were never returned after the war. This is about more than art, Gabriella."

He reached into his jacket, producing a small envelope. "There's a package waiting for you at your flat. Your flight to Paris leaves tonight."

Gabriella's eyes narrowed. "And what makes you think I'll

help you?"

"Because" Moshe leaned in, his voice low, "your family name is on the list. And there's another piece, something from Israel, stolen long ago. It's resurfaced and is being auctioned off in Paris."

Gabriella's heart pounded, but she maintained her composure. "And you expect me to just"

"You don't have much time," Moshe interrupted. "We'll talk before your flight." He stood, placing a gentle kiss on her forehead before walking out of the restaurant.

Gabriella sat there for a moment; the weight of his words settled in.

CHAPTER 26

Game On

Abdel didn't return to his flat after working a grueling shift. Fatigue weighed on him heavily, and all he wanted was to collapse into sleep, but instead of retreating home, he found solace in the open air of the Tuileries Garden. The evening Parisian sunbathed the park, where groups of people lazed on benches, grass, and chairs—something that felt oddly safe and liberating in this city. Abdel lay on a bench, letting the world blur as sleep took him, except for his phone alarm going off that reminded him of the football game.

He ran his fingers through his wiry hair, trying to smooth it down as best he could before heading to the metro. His friends awaited him at a local bar, the type of place where the cheap beer flowed freely than conversation, and most patrons had stories of struggle. Immigrants like Abdel, Mohammed (now simply "Mo"), and Yasin filled the dimly lit space. Their jobs were menial— janitors, street cleaners, and the occasional taxi driver—but they all shared one thing: survival.

The bar buzzed with energy as fans cheered on their respective teams, the air thick with tension and the redolence of stale beer. Abdel found his friends guarding two bar stools in the corner, where they greeted him with the usual ribbing for his tardiness and disheveled appearance. They exchanged hugs and laughed about how Abdel had "rolled straight out of bed" before ordering another round.

The game was slow to start, but as players tired, substitutions brought fresh energy to the field. Abdel got caught up in the excitement, almost forgetting about the key cards in his pocket until he reached for his wallet.

"Hey, what's that?" Mo, quick with his hands and even quicker with his questions, had spotted the cards before Abdel could shove them back into his coat. Abdel froze as Mo plucked them from his grip.

"They look important," Mo said, inspecting them. "You get a promotion, Abdel?"

The group erupted in laughter. The idea that Abdel—an immigrant janitor—be entrusted with security access to the Palais was absurd. Yet, there was something ominous in the way the group studied the cards. Yasin, a sharp-witted chemical engineering student whose father was a diplomat, eyed them with care. His father disapproved of his friendships, especially with these men. It made Yasin cling to them even more, enjoying the defiance.

"You sure you're not in trouble, Abdel?" asked Omar, the tall, lanky guy who, despite working at a sanitary office, had been blessed with a desk job. Similar to the rest, he was cheap labor, filling a gap in France's economy that no one else wanted to.

"I just forgot to return them," Abdel mumbled, trying to find the right words. He didn't want them to think he was a thief. He could be cast out of their circle faster than a finger swipe on Tinder.

"Wait, you could show us around the Palais later!" Mo joked, though the glimmer in his eyes suggested he wasn't entirely joking.

They all groaned at Mo's suggestion, mocking the absurdity of their luck with women. "Even if we tried Tinder, we wouldn't get anywhere," Yasin quipped, and the group erupted in laughter.

As the group passed the cards around, discussing how the magnetic strip must unlock doors in some high-security way beyond their education, they almost didn't see the well-dressed man coming closer. Trim, with a slight British accent and a carefully groomed beard, he seemed out of place in the bar's rugged, immigrant ambiance.

"Good evening, gentlemen," the man said, his gaze falling on Yasin. "Ambassador Kader's son, isn't it? We met at Global Giving last year, didn't we?"

Yasin blinked, struggling to place the man. He'd attended the fundraiser but had little interest in the people there, attending out of obligation to his father.

"My name is Youssef Samara, but please, call me Yosie," the man continued, his tone warm but with an underlying sense of control. His grip was firm, hands rough—too rough for a mere philanthropist.

The friends exchanged glances, unsure what to make of this well-dressed stranger. They had encountered many people from their homeland in Paris, but never someone like Yosie, someone who had power and influence.

Yosie had been watching them, or more accurately, stalking them. He tracked their every move, their routines, their struggles.

Perhaps his voice was friendly, but his intentions set far from benign. He was calculating, studying them like pawns in a larger game.

"Hope your father's well," Yosie offered, his eyes still on Yasin, who shifted uncomfortably under the weight of the man's attention.

"Uh, yeah. He's in Belgium right now," Yasin replied, still unsure who this man was or what he wanted.

Yosie smiled, knowing full well the ambassador was out of the country. He had done his homework. These men were isolated, clinging to each other for a sense of belonging, surviving in a country that tolerated them but never fully embraced them. This bar, this football game, was a rare break from their reality— a reality that Yosie was about to shatter.

"May I join you?" Yosie asked, more of a statement than a question.

The group, caught off guard, offered no resistance. Yosie ordered additional round of drinks and seamlessly integrated himself into their conversations—about discrimination, politics, and girls. He cheered louder than anyone else during the game, his presence commanding their attention.

But beneath the camaraderie, Abdel couldn't shake the feeling that something was off. The way Yosie's eyes lingered on Yasin, the subtle shifts in his body language—everything about him felt orchestrated. And as the night wore on, Abdel's unease grew, though he couldn't quite pinpoint why.

The game ended with little fanfare, but the night's real game had only just begun.

CHAPTER 27

Yosie's Proposition

The bar buzzed with energy, and Yosie held court, captivating the group with tales of his travels across the Asian islands off Vietnam. His stories, woven with intrigue and eroticism, held the young men in thrall. Despite the alcohol loosening their tongues, it was Yosie's genuine charm that made them feel at ease, finding a strange comfort in the company of the mysterious man.

As the night deepened, Abdel, leaning in, asked the question that lingered in the back of his mind. "So, sorry for asking, but... what's your connection to my dad?"

A bold question, one made braver by the drink, and for a moment, the table fell into an awkward silence. But Yosie, showing no sign of offense, just smiled. He leaned back, seemingly unbothered, before launching into a story that blended truth with finely crafted deception. He spoke of his time with the Syrian military and of Abdel's father's ventures in Lebanon.

The truth, however, was veiled beneath layers of manipulation. He painted a picture of a man who made a fortune exploiting cheap labor in southern Lebanon, exporting olive oil while secretly running arms to the West Bank and Syria. Rumors of a scandal circulated— honey traps and underage girls — that might have destroyed Abdel's father and his entire family. But his father escaped, becoming an ambassador, a man forever beholden to the Syrian regime, smuggling money across borders under the guise of diplomatic immunity.

The young men, intoxicated by both the alcohol and Yosie's tales, hung onto every word, unaware of the deep, dark layers beneath the surface. By the time the bar closed, they were begging to meet Yosie again, urging him to join them at the disco the upcoming night. They half-joked about his prowess with women, taunting him into coming along.

Yosie smiled, placing a hefty arm around Abdel's shoulders. "I'd like that very much," he said. His voice was calm yet appeared a certain weight to it that Abdel couldn't quite place. Then, leaning closer, Yosie added, "But first, I have a proposition. Walk with me, will you?"

The group exchanged glances, laughing off any suspicions. "You're safer with him than on your own tonight," one of the guys called out as they parted ways. The streets had grown dangerous for immigrants lately, especially with tensions high across Europe. French nationalists and hooligans had taken to beating anyone they deemed foreign. Abdel, feeling a mixture of relief and curiosity, followed Yosie into the night.

The air outside was cutting and cool, a contrast to the stifling warmth of the bar. The distant drone of Seine and the muted glow of the streetlamps created a serene, almost otherworldly atmosphere as they walked. Yosie, in a seemingly casual manner, brought up the key cards Abdel had in his possession.

"They're probably useless by now, right?" Yosie said, his tone light. "I bet they've been reported missing, access revoked.

But I'm still interested. I'll give you a year's worth of salary for them."

Abdel blinked, the offer hitting him like a jolt of electricity. Those cards had been a source of stress — he'd feared losing his job over them. But now, Yosie was offering a way out, a way to make lots of money than he could dream of, all for something that he believed was now worthless.

"Tomorrow night," Abdel responded, in a steady voice. "I'll bring the cards an hour before we meet the others."

Yosie smiled, a smile that didn't quite reach his eyes. "Perfect."

As they neared the Metro station, the realization hit them both that the trains had stopped for the night. The late hour and the government's austerity measures had brought public transport to a halt. Abdel apologized profusely, promising to meet Yosie earlier the following night. They parted ways, Yosie vanishing into the darkness of the Latin Quarter as Abdel headed home, his thoughts racing.

The night air cleared Abdel's head. A peculiar sense of happiness washed over him, like a weight had been lifted from his shoulders. The sale of the cards allowed him to ignore the consequences and move forward. His steps quickened as he walked along the Seine, cutting through narrow alleyways towards his flat. The streets mostly empty, save for the occasional street cleaner, their hoses spraying water onto the cobblestone roads.

As Abdel approached the Jardin Alpin, he didn't notice the shadow that slipped silently from the side street, moving with a deadly precision. It wasn't until he felt the biting steel against his flesh that he realized something was terribly wrong.

The pain hit him like a freight train, sharp and searing, radiating from his stomach up into his chest. His body trembled, his knees buckling beneath him, but he couldn't fall. His hand instinctively reached down, finding a knife hilt buried deep in his abdomen, and then he saw Yosie's face, calm and expressionless, looming above him.

Yosie's movements were methodical, precise. The Fairbairn-Sykes knife he carried was designed for close-quarters combat, a tool of death. As Abdel's body gave out, Yosie pulled the knife free, quickly wiping the blade clean on Abdel's shirt before reaching into his victim's pocket to retrieve the key cards.

Abdel's eyes, once full of life, stared blankly into the night. His breath rattled in his throat; It was almost impossible to hear over the distant hum of the street cleaners.

Yosie said a quiet prayer, a ritual he performed more out of habit than belief, before pushing Abdel's lifeless body into the shadows of the alley. He knew the street cleaners wouldn't find the body for a while — they always took their break near the pizzeria, smoking and chatting about the mundane details of their lives.

With the cards secured and his blade clean, Yosie vanished into the night. His thoughts already turning to the following phase of the operation. The auction was tomorrow, and with these key cards, he could explore parts of the museum that even the ambassador's tickets wouldn't grant access to.

As he disappeared into the labyrinth of Paris' streets, Yosie couldn't help but think how well everything had played out. The ambassador, his son, and their circle of young friends were all expendable, mere pawns in a larger game. Months of planning had gone into this heist, and now everything was falling into place.

Tomorrow, he would watch the greatest art theft in history unfold, its true perpetrator will remain a mystery. The group he worked for didn't need recognition; they thrived in the shadows, covertly funding the terrorist groups that shook the world. But unlike those radicals, Yosie's employers had no interest in making loud statements. They remain the ones pulling the strings, orchestrating chaos for profit.

And Yosie, like the blade he carried, was their sharpest weapon.

CHAPTER 28

Alleys of Paris

Like a shadow, Yoise's movements were unnoticeable, sticking to the narrow, shadowy alleys that wound through the heart of Paris. His every step calculated, he avoided the wide boulevards, where CCTV cameras blinked like unblinking eyes. The city slept, but danger never rested. After an hour of twisting through these serpentine streets, he pulled out his burner phone and dialed.

"ID number?" A curt, mechanical voice answered.

Yoise recited the sequence of digits etched on the stolen museum card. The silence on the line stretched taut, was filled solely with the ambient hum of the city. Finally, the voice instructed him to call back in thirty minutes.

Perfect. Time enough to blend in. He ducked into a kebab stand near the Centre Pompidou, where the scent of charred meat and garlic mingled with the damp chill of the night. The vendor, oblivious, served Yoise while a group of local police officers stood nearby, chatting idly about the night's patrol. Unemployed men loitered in the park across the street, watching the world pass them by, just as the officers did.

Yoise took a bite of his kebab, savoring the flavors as he checked the time. Forty-five minutes passed before he called back. This time, the hacker had good news.

"Address: Rue de Buenos Ayres, number 5. Borot Chartrand, lives alone. No known relatives. Balance of 150,000 euros in his account."

Yoise's lips curled. Chartrand's apartment wasn't far from the Eiffel Tower. He could get there in less than fifteen minutes. He slid his phone into his jacket and began walking, his pace casual but focused. The light of the Eiffel Tower loomed in the distance, casting a pale glow over the Seine as if guiding him to his next mark.

The entrance to Chartrand's building was tucked discreetly behind a café. Yoise tested the back door—locked, as expected. But this wasn't a movie where he'd tediously pick the lock. Instead, he crouched, positioned his shoulder just beneath the knob, and took a deep breath. On the exhale, he drove his weight into the door. The wood splintered, and the door swung unbarred with a dull crack. He waited, listening for any signs of disturbance inside the building. Nothing.

He moved into the dim hallway, the faint buzz of a single, weak bulb hanging near the mail slots. There were four apartments in total, one belonging to Chartrand on the third floor. The other, to a woman named Ms. Jones. Noted.

The stairs creaked softly underfoot, but Yoise's movements were smooth, practiced. At 4:30 a.m., the city would soon stir. He had no time to waste.

Chartrand's flat was conveniently located at the back of the building, close to the fire escape. Breaking this door would risk waking Ms. Jones, so Yoise opted for a quieter route. He approached the window adjacent to the stairwell. No curtains.

Chartrand was a careless man, it seemed.

Inside, Chartrand tossed and turned, a restless sleeper. The old man kicked off his blankets in frustration, muttering curses under his breath. Yoise waited, his breath steady, his pulse slow. Ten minutes passed before Chartrand dragged himself out of bed and shuffled to the bathroom.

Yoise moved with a single, sharp tap of his knife, he shattered the glass of the window, quietly reaching inside to unlock it. With the noiseless tread of a wraith, he appeared, his boots softly touching the aged floor.

Books lay scattered everywhere, piles of magazines stacked against the walls, and journals littering the bed—each one a testament to Chartrand's obsession with the museum.

The curator-in-waiting. Yoise smiled faintly.

In the bathroom, Chartrand sighed, glaring at the reflection of his sagging face. His nightly trips to relieve his swollen prostate had become a bitter ritual. He grumbled to himself, waved dismissively at the mirror, and flushed the toilet.

He walked into the kitchen, craving a cool drink to soothe his insomnia. As he reached for the fridge door, something made him pause—a cool draft brushing against his bare legs. His gaze drifted to the open window.

A chill spread through him, colder than the night air.

In an instant, Yoise was upon him. His left arm wrapped around Chartrand's face, yanking his head back with brutal efficiency. The knife plunged into Chartrand's back, just beneath the shoulder blade. The blade tore through his lung with surgical precision. Chartrand gasped, his legs buckling, his body flailing as if caught in a vicious spasm.

The older man's brain struggled to process the pain. His mind, confused, thought he was suffering a heart attack. But his heart was intact—the damage was far more lethal. Yoise held him steady, watching him writhe, listening to the wheezing gurgles as blood filled Chartrand's lungs. Five agonizing minutes passed before the man's body gave out. The final thought flickering through Chartrand's mind was a fleeting regret that he'd never become curator.

Yoise knelt beside the corpse, cleaning his blade with methodical calm. There was no rush, no panic. The sun's first light crept over the rooftops, casting extended shadows as the city of Paris began to awaken.

He climbed out the window as the sky brightened, his work done. Fingerprints weren't a concern him—he wasn't in any database. He vanished down the fire escape, disappearing into the city's morning bustle. Five was the scheduled start time for the Metro, and by then, Yoise would be long gone, just another ghost in the city of light.

And Chartrand? He was already forgotten.

Yoise's mission had just begun, and Paris would soon feel the ripple effect of his lethal efficiency. The proceeding steps involved far more than blood; they involved power, wealth, and the ancient artifacts that held the key to destabilizing greater than just a city—but entire nations.

CHAPTER 29

Tel Aviv

Gabriella moved silently through the narrow streets of Tel Aviv, ever mindful of the shadows and potential eyes. As she approached her flat, A faint familiarity tingled within her—a sense of being watched. It wasn't paranoia. Years in the Israeli security force had ingrained in her the instincts of surveillance and counter-surveillance. She knew the security blanket around her was tighter than ever, despite having officially left the service. Unofficially, she was still in the game.

The door creaked as she entered, and the alarm system flashed green as she disabled it. But her eyes fell instantly on a large, government-sealed envelope lying in the hallway. Its presence, both expected and unnerving, suggested this mission was different. She couldn't afford distractions, not now.

She carried the envelope to the kitchen, the weight of it promising a burden she hadn't anticipated. With a deep breath, Gabriella picked up a steak knife, sliced through the seal, and unfolded the package's contents. Inside three thick folders, along with a handwritten note clipped to the top.

The note read: "This could not be done without your experience, and for that, the Israeli government thanks you—so do I. While you're in Paris, bring me back some sweets from Boulangerie Murciano, will you?" Pappy

The corner of her mouth lifted into a little smile. Even in the middle of a crisis, Pappy's thinking about food. It was a kosher bakery in the heart of Paris, a relic from the Jewish quarter. But the humor faded as she realized the gravity of the assignment.

The files contained photos of stolen artwork and artifacts—pieces that had disappeared decades ago, during the chaos of the Nazi occupation. Many belonged to Jewish families, including her own. Gabriella's heart sank as she thumbed through images of items that should have been returned to their rightful owners. Instead hidden away in the vast labyrinth of Europe's black market. The mission's significance was deeply personal.

There was one piece that stood out—a cylindrical artifact with Hebrew inscriptions. It triggered something in her memory, a fragment of a conversation with her late grandfather about a rare object stolen from their family during the war. She couldn't quite place it, but the sense of connection left her unsettled.

Focus, she told herself.

She spent two hours committing the details to memory—images, serial numbers, hotel addresses, and agent contacts. The cylinder weighed heavily on her mind. Burn bag in hand, she made her way to the small fire pit on her terrace, the sound of the crackling paper oddly soothing in the warm Tel Aviv night. As the files turned to ash, Gabriella steeled herself. This mission wasn't just another operation; it was deeply tied to her family's past. The art wasn't just valuable—it was a symbol of lives destroyed; stories erased.

With the final ember fading, she packed her bag. She chose her attire with precision—formal enough for Parisian events, but not flashy. Stella McCartney worked. As always, her shoes were sensible. If she needed to run, she wouldn't let vanity slow her down.

Memories of her initial Parisian mission entered her mind, a rookie mistake almost exposing her. Lost in the streets, she had forgotten her agent's number. How could she have been so green? Her team had rescued her, but they never let her forget it. Little Eiffel Tower keychains appeared in her bags or left on her desk as a constant reminder.

Not this time, she thought. This time, no room for error.

Flight from Tel Aviv

Gabriella's 4 pm flight was booked on El Al, where security was paramount. The intense screening procedures meant there was no room for surprises, a comfort Gabriella appreciated. Still, the smell of fried dough and sugary Danishes in the crew lounge turned her stomach. She reached for a bottle of water, trying to ignore the bustling crowd and the nervous energy that airports always seemed to breed.

When her flight was eventually called, she passed through the gate. A family of five in front of her struggled with their excitable child, a girl no older than five, pulling on her mother's arm and asking the same question repeatedly. "Are we going now, Mommy?" The mother's patience visibly waned, and Gabriella couldn't help but smirk. Some missions are harder than others, she mused.

After handing over her boarding pass, the gate agent smiled. "You're in business class. No need to worry about sitting next to them," she said, nodding toward the family. Gabriella offered a polite smile and headed down the ramp.

As she reached her seat, a window seat in the business class cabin, she noticed an elderly woman fast asleep in the aisle seat adjacent to her. Gabriella maneuvered around her carefully, settling into her seat, her thoughts already preoccupied with the mission. But just as she was about to immerse herself in the details, a voice jolted her back to the present.

"Pardon me, bubbie," a thick Australian accent drawled. "I think that's my seat next to you."

The elderly woman stirred, grunting as she shuffled out of her seat to let the man through. Gabriella's eyes flickered toward the newcomer—tall, blonde, and unmistakably Australian, with the laid-back swagger of a surfer who had somehow stumbled into business class. His backpack was tattered, held together precariously with twine, and stickers from all over the world covered its surface.

As he plopped into his seat, the man smiled broadly at Gabriella. "G'day! You don't mind if I play some tunes, do ya? Helps with the nerves," adjusting his headphones.

Of course, an Australian surfer with flight anxiety. Gabriella suppressed an eye roll. The last thing she needed was a chatty seatmate during her flight to Paris. She had plenty to think about—too much at stake. But before she could respond, the Aussie was already lost in his music, air-guitaring enthusiastically.

Gabriella sighed, turning toward the window. The artwork she was tasked with recovering was stolen property and stolen history, a legacy that needed to be reclaimed. Her grandparents had fought for years to get back what was taken from them during the war. Now it was her fight.

As the plane lifted off the tarmac, the Australian turned to her again, this time with a softer tone. "Sorry, is it too loud? I get a bit antsy before takeoff."

Gabriella's lips twitched into a reluctant smile. "It's fine," she muttered, redirected her attention to the window.

CHAPTER 30

Paris

Stone felt the weight of the city pressing in as they emerged from the labyrinthine metro tunnels into the heart of Paris. The warm afternoon light, diffused by the towering buildings, cast lengthy shadows across the streets, bringing with it a mixture of nostalgia and unease. Catherine, still clutching the map, glanced at Stone with furrowed brows.

"Are we lost?" she asked, her Midwestern drawl laced with frustration.

Stone didn't answer immediately. He scanned the street, his eyes darting from face to face, calculating, assessing. He couldn't shake the feeling of being watched, however nothing overt. Still, his instincts were honed. The weight of the backpack increased with each passing moment. It wasn't just the physical weight; it was the significance of its contents. The stolen artwork, the artifacts—items tied to a dark history, their true value far beyond monetary. Those keys unlocked untold secrets.

He checked his watch—3 p.m. Paris time. He had just an hour before most banks closed, and he had to find a secure depository. There was no room for error. Two locations in the vicinity, both vetted during his flight. He pulled Catherine by the arm, his voice low but firm.

"I need to take care of something first," leading her toward the Seine.

As they moved through the bustling streets, the aroma of freshly baked pastries and coffee wafted through the air, mingling with the faint, metallic tang of the river. Stone's senses remain on high alert, every sound, every shift in the air cataloged. The hum of Paris around him—the laughter of tourists, the murmur of French conversation—felt too normal. Too calm. It put him on edge.

Catherine, oblivious to the undercurrents of tension, played the role of tourist, gazing at the vibrant green stalls along the riverbanks, filled with aged books, records, and trinkets. But Stone's mind was elsewhere. They were nearing Point Zéro, the literal heart of France. It was crowded with tourists, a perfect spot to disappear.

Notre Dame loomed before them, a towering Gothic masterpiece, its spires casting deep shadows across the square. Stone paused, taking in the sight for a moment, the weight of history pressing down on him.

"You ever been here?" Catherine asked, her voice soft, awe evident in her tone.

"Once," he replied, his eyes scanning the crowd, looking for anything—anyone—out of place. The more people, the easier it was to blend in. But the stakes were high, and every second mattered. "Stay here. Play tourist for thirty minutes. I need to secure this."

He gestured to the backpack, the casualness of the motion belying the gravity of the situation. Stolen artwork wasn't all the bag contained. It held pieces of history that never should have been lost in the first place, artifacts from Jewish families taken during the German occupation of France. The courts had dragged their feet for decades, hoping the claimants would fade away. Most did. Stone's grandparents never saw justice. But that's why this mission was personal.

Catherine smiled, trying to mask her nerves. "You better come back. You're not leaving me here alone with the street urchins," she teased, though there was a flicker of genuine concern in her eyes.

Though already thinking of his upcoming move, a faint chuckle came from Stone.

"I'll be back. Promise." He kissed her cheek and gave her a playful push toward the cathedral. "Don't get into trouble."

He turned sharply, his pace quickening as he made his way through the narrow, cobblestone streets. The weight of the backpack increased against his back, as though the ghosts of the stolen objects inside were demanding justice.

The alley he entered was more of a pedestrian lane, lined with small shops and cafes. No cars, only people. Perfect. He paused at a storefront, pretending to admire a display of artisanal cheeses, but his eyes flicked to the glass reflection, scanning for tails. No one. Still, his pulse quickened.

Ten minutes later, he reached his destination: a nondescript building on Rue Daubenton, overshadowed by the towering Grande Mosquée de Paris across the street. Its plain exterior and subtle signage belied its importance. Stone approached the door, glancing up at the security camera nestled in the trees, its lens aimed directly at him.

A buzz sounded, and the massive metal door clicked unlocked. Stone stepped inside, right away aware of the subtle scent of fresh paint mixed with something colder—sterile. This place had excessive security; more than your average bank. But that's why he'd chosen it.

The entryway was thick, reinforced. Metal detectors, scanners—nothing was left to chance. As Stone moved deeper into the building, he heard the murmur of French conversation from a distant office, the clacking of heels on the marble floors, and the faint whir of cameras tracking his movements.

A woman appeared from a side room; behind rimless glasses, her eyes were sharp. Her hair was pulled back into a tight bun, her tailored suit pristine. Everything about her screamed efficiency.

"Good afternoon," she greeted him in flawless French. Her tone was polite, professional. But Stone saw through the façade. She wanted this over as quick as possible. No warmth in her smile, only the mechanics of courtesy.

"I'm here to open a depository," Stone replied, handing over his credentials. "I emailed ahead."

The woman, whose name tag read Cynthia Clpoeria, took the documents without a word. Her fingers moved deftly across a tablet as she processed his request.

"Of course, Doctor Stone. We've been expecting you," she said, glancing at the clock. It was almost closing time. Her impatience was palpable, though expertly concealed beneath layers of professionalism.

She led him down a corridor to a room dominated by an

ornate wooden desk—a relic from another time. The juxtaposition of the antique furniture and the modern security measures didn't escape Stone. It was designed to impress, to create an illusion of old-world trust. But Stone wasn't here for the ambiance. He was here to hide something no one could afford to lose.

As he sat down and opened his backpack, the weight of what he was about to do settled over him. This wasn't just a routine drop-off. The stolen artwork and artifacts in that bag were greater than historical treasures. They were the final remnants of lives destroyed, of families erased. And now, they remain Stone's responsibility.

CHAPTER 31

The Depository

Stone completed his business with efficiency, spending less than three minutes inside the vault's cubicle. The woman at the desk was nearly oblivious to how fast he proceeded, more relieved that he hadn't delayed her evening plans. Stepping from the bank, the weight of the key card and bank ID in his pocket brought a faint sense of accomplishment, but his mind remained on high alert.

Emerging into the brisk Parisian afternoon, Stone crossed Boulevard du Palais, his senses fine-tuned for any sign of pursuit. The narrow alleyways of the city, like arteries, pulsed with life yet provided shadowed crevices for those who knew them well. He ducked into a souvenir shop, feigning interest in trinkets for just a heartbeat before moving straight toward the back, where the unassuming storage room awaited.

The faint scent of dust and neglected inventory lingered as he startled the napping store clerk. Before the man fully registered Stone's presence, he had vanished through the employee exit, slipping into an alley so narrow the walls almost grazed his shoulders. He was aware that if anyone was tailing him, this was where they'd close in. His heart pounded in rhythm with his quickening steps, though outwardly he remained calm, his face a mask of nonchalance.

Every muscle was tense, prepared for confrontation, but his gamble paid off—he emerged onto Rue Dante. Stone scanned the street, making sure to avoid direct eye contact with the few passersby. He crossed entering La Banque Postale, knowing full well the establishment didn't offer safety deposit boxes. It was all part of the misdirection. The cameras tracking his every move capturing this stop, and he needed them to.

After exchanging large euros for smaller bills, he made his way back toward Catherine. Forty minutes had passed, and he found her exactly where he had left her—by the cathedral, her attention fixed on a group of teenagers performing tricks on their skateboards.

The skateboards clattered against the stone plaza, echoing off the ancient walls of Notre Dame. The air carried a mix of history and the faint scent of the river. Stone came near without a sound, his gaze sweeping over the square, scanning for anything out of place, anyone who might have taken a large amount of interest in them.

"Why the long face?" Stone's voice broke through Catherine's concentration, startling her as he gently bumped her arm.

She turned, her expression a mix of frustration and amusement. "Can you believe it? Closed. Some private event for a cardinal or bishop. I didn't catch all the details; the guard was too busy staring down my shirt."

Stone smirked, He paid little attention to the comment. His attention was divided between Catherine and the crowd, his instincts still humming with caution. "Overrated anyway," he replied casually, already moving toward her suitcase. He wanted to get them out in the open and into their upcoming destination.

"Where are we staying?"

Stone gestured toward Hotel La Fant Palaces, an imposing edifice standing like a sentinel among the older subdued buildings. "Right there."

The hotel was as grand as it was discreet, built in 1722 and steeped in centuries of royal and diplomatic history. Its splendor appealed solely to the wealthiest. those whose power and influence shielded them from the prying eyes of the world. Stone preferred it that way. The higher the exclusivity, the more layers of security, the easier it was for him to blend into the shadows.

As they entered the lobby, Stone's gaze darted from the extravagant flower arrangements to the sweeping marble floors, up to the vaulted ceilings that seemed to stretch endlessly. But his mind was elsewhere, cataloging the exits, noting the placement of cameras, and mentally marking the positions of security personnel. Their roles went beyond that of doormen, and their builds suggested backgrounds in something far more physical than hospitality.

Catherine, by contrast, was visibly entranced by the grandeur. Her wide-eyed expression and soft murmurs of awe made her seem almost out of place among the polished marble and antique furniture. Stone couldn't afford to let his guard down, not even for a moment. The world around him was a tapestry of potential threats, and every detail was a thread he needed to keep track of.

Midway through the lobby, Stone's heart skipped a beat. His

eyes locked onto a man seated in an oversized chair, flanked by two bodyguards. The blond man's sunglasses reflected the light just enough to obscure his eyes, but Stone recognized the subtle gesture—the slight flick of his hand toward someone seated nearby, a figure angled away from view. However, it was not the man that caught his attention. It was the woman seated across from him. Her tan complexion, the elegant curve of her legs crossed casually, the pumps, and most damningly—the tiny, horseshoe-shaped scar behind her left knee.

It was her.

The scar, not noticeable to most, was unforgettable to Stone. He had placed it there himself, years ago, during a mission that had gone sideways. A shard of metal, embedded dangerously close to an artery, removed in a moment of improvised battlefield surgery.

He pulled Catherine off to the side, trying to gain a better view without drawing attention, but a bodyguard moved, his broad back obstructing Stone's line of sight.

Catherine, oblivious to the tension, squeezed Stone's hand and smiled up at him. "Thank you."

"For what?" Stone replied, his voice distant as he tried to process the implications of what he had just seen.

"For this," Catherine gestured around. "It's been so long since I had a proper vacation."

Stone forced a smile. "Don't thank me yet. Wait until you see the room. You might change your mind."

"I doubt that" she laughed, her mood light as she pulled her suitcase along the cobblestones toward the reception desk.

Stone's mind, however, was racing. The woman—was she here for him? And the man? He had to confirm their identities, but it couldn't happen here, not out in the open.

At the reception, a thin, owl-eyed man in his 30s greeted them, his formal attire meticulously kept, though his demeanor lacked warmth.

"Good afternoon, Monsieur and Mademoiselle. Your name?"

"Stone."

The man's fingers clicked across the keyboard. "Ah, yes, Dr. Stone. Suite 1602, one of our finest, overlooking the dome. I'm sure you'll find it quite... accommodating."

As they ascended to their room, Stone's thoughts remained anchored in the lobby. He had to know if she had seen him—if she even remembered him. For now, though, he had to act calm to avoid raising suspicion.

The suite was as lavish as promised, with panoramic views of the Palais Dome and the gardens below. Catherine marveled at the sight, already snapping pictures from the balcony, while Stone remained inside, unwilling to expose himself to potential threats.

He watched her silhouette, carefree in the fading daylight, and forced his mind to relax—just for a moment. But the woman in the lobby wasn't leaving his thoughts. If she was here, so was trouble. The kind of trouble that didn't let loose ends dangle.

CHAPTER 32

Lebanon 1999

The relentless breeze from the Mediterranean Sea did little to dissipate the overwhelming stench of the makeshift refugee camp. Human waste and garbage piled two stories high in the outskirts of Beirut's southern suburbs, under Hezbollah's control, creating a nauseating, ever-present reminder of the dire conditions. By midday, the scorching sun beat down on the camp's 800 occupants—displaced Christian Lebanese, Turks, Palestinians, and additional ethnic groups rejected by the Shi'a majority. Among them - 400 children, elderly, and sick individuals, huddled under tattered tents. As the wind shifted inland, the temperature spiked to 125 degrees, amplifying the tension in the air. Tempers flared, and the sounds of nearby gunfire and artillery explosions punctuated the oppressive heat like a death knell.

The camp, an unsettling mélange of suffering and desperation, stood trapped between factions. Regime forces sealed the nomads in, their escape routes cut off, leaving them with dwindling food, medicine, and hope. The burst of automatic gunfire, once terrifying, had become routine. The distant explosions, remain an unsettling reminder that death might strike from the sky at any moment. Shells from artillery barrages would sometimes land dangerously close, rattling the thin walls of their canvas shelters, making even the strongest quake with fear.

At the heart of the camp, a large tent masqueraded as a hospital. It wasn't much—a ten-by-fifteen-meter structure acting as a fragile sanctuary for the ill and injured. Inside, an international team of doctors toiled, led by a Swiss surgeon, Sebastian, a towering figure with hawkish features and hands too large for the delicate work he performed. His professors had once doubted his ability as a surgeon, but now those oversized hands routinely saved lives, performing precise operations in the middle of chaos. His blond hair and cold blue eyes mirrored the icy precision with which he navigated his tasks. He had long sought adventure, and the exotic Middle East, once romanticized in his mind, had become a crucible of horrors he now confronted daily.

Sebastian, however, wasn't alone in this mission. The medical team, consisting of a Swiss, Italian, French, German, and an American—who passed himself off as Canadian—formed a motley crew of specialists. Each of them had their reasons for being here, but one had a hidden agenda that had yet to unfold. They received a generous amount of money, far greater than typical humanitarian workers, which made their presence even more questionable. Who was paying them? The answers were buried in layers of geopolitics and revenge plots, the real motives shrouded in secrecy.

The true patron of this operation was a wealthy Saudi. His sister had died in this very camp while working as a volunteer, and while his public mission was to continue her charitable work, his private objective was far darker: revenge. A different doctor shared that same thirst for vengeance, a secret known to only a handful of people. This secret connection added another dangerous layer to an already volatile situation, where the shifting desert winds mirror the instability of alliances.

The warlord of southern Lebanon, Colonel Hajj Multicki, loomed over the region like a malevolent specter. A former smuggler, he had grown rich on the blood and chaos of civil war, amassing power through illicit arms deals with jihadists, Al Qaeda, and anyone else willing to pay his price. His ambition knew no bounds, as he steadily pushed the Lebanese army back to the sea, claiming added territory with every conflict. Multicki's men, hardened and ruthless, frequently required medical attention. They summon the doctors from the camp, knowing that refusal was not an option. And when his wounded men could no longer be saved, Multicki often finish them off himself—a grim reminder to anyone who dared defy him.

Sebastian despised being summoned to treat these war criminals, but there was little choice. Like the rest of the medical team, he lived under the watchful eye of Hezbollah. The doctors were prisoners in all but name, unable to leave the camp without an armed escort. The pretext was their safety, but they knew better—being watched, controlled, and manipulated, just like everyone else in this war-torn land.

Despite the oppressive conditions, the American doctor— a broad-shouldered, athletic man in his late twenties with wavy brown hair and gentle green eyes—managed to maintain an air of optimism. His carefree grin belied the horrors he had witnessed, and he spent majority of his time playing with the children, teaching them to walk again after the IEDs had taken their limbs. He turned their rehabilitation into a game, distracting them from the grim reality of their surroundings. His charm and youthful arrogance rubbed some of his colleagues the wrong way, but his heart was in the right place. He was a beacon of hope, albeit a flawed one, in a place that seemed devoid of it.

His actions did not go unnoticed inside and out of the compound. Local store owners would stuff more food or supplies in his duffle bag when he enters the city. A number of times he meet with a smuggler with an Israeli passport for harder to find items. The smuggler's name was David. Stone evaded the guards and move on his own outside the perimeter of the camp. Resulting in the arm goons shooting their automatic weapons in the air when he returned. He meet their murderess eyes with contempt. Stone's larger size and height did not take the idle threat seriously, the doctors chastised him for the provocation. He laughed it off and profess, "the bread is freshest in the early mornings, and I like to be first in line for the baker's daughter is worth the effort."

The staff would say out loud he was an arrogant young American and take his contraband and return to their work. Except Gabriella, the French doctor with dark hair and penetrating brown eyes, was a stark contrast to the American. Tall, lean, and strong, she moved with a feline grace that turned heads wherever she went. Her beauty was impossible to ignore, especially in the close confines of the camp, but she wielded it as a shield, deflecting unwanted attention with ease. The guards leered at her when she passed, but she played their game, exaggerating her movements just enough to keep them off balance. She disappeared often, slipping from camp for reasons she never disclosed, returning without explanation.

Despite their differences, there was an unspoken bond between Gabriella and the American, forged through the shared trials of war. He teased her relentlessly, particularly during her morning workouts, but beneath the banter, could be found mutual respect. Both of them carried burdens they rarely spoke of, yet they found solace in each other's company, if only for fleeting moments.

The camp existed in a state of uneasy tension; a fragile bubble of life surrounded by death. Every day brought new challenges, threats, and opportunities for betrayal. The doctors, trapped in this web of war and politics, clung to their missions, but the clock was ticking. One of them had a deadline to meet, a secret agenda that might change everything, and the longer they stayed, the more dangerous their situation became.

As the sun dipped below the horizon, casting long shadows over the camp, Sebastian stood at the entrance of the hospital tent, his eyes scanning the perimeter. He was certain about tonight, like every other night, the sounds of gunfire and explosions served as a grim lullaby. But beneath the surface, something else was brewing. Enemies encircled them as alliances changed, and the time for action was running out.

CHAPTER 33

Beirut New Year's Eve

The cool Mediterranean breeze was deceptive, failing to mask the oppressive stench of the refugee camp. The mixture of rotting garbage, human waste, and despair clung to the air, pervasive and unyielding. Under Hezbollah's control, the southern outskirts of Beirut were a powder keg, but tonight, it was New Year's Eve. The doctors, weary from months of tending to the sick and wounded, had decided to indulge themselves with a brief respite—an evening in the city, escaping the misery that had swallowed their days whole.

Colonel Hajj Multicki, the self-proclaimed warlord of southern Lebanon, had agreed to their request for a night out, offering his "protection" with a sly grin that never reached his eyes. His henchman, Antwan, delivered the news with hardly concealed contempt, eyes flickering to Gabriella as he spoke, lingering a beat too long. "Don't worry," Antwan said, his voice oily, "everything's arranged. The Colonel's finest will escort you. A car, food, drink—the best the Middle East has to offer. Maybe more, if you wish." His gaze, predatory, slid over Gabriella's form with shameless intent.

Gabriella, unfazed, met his stare with a cool smile, shifting her weight seductively, one hip cocked as she eyed the soldier. "I hope the Colonel himself will join us. It would be such a disappointment if he didn't."

Antwan's smirk faltered for a moment, replaced by a glimmer of unease. "Depends on his master's wishes," he muttered, his gaze shifting as if uncertain of Gabriella's true intentions.

The American, Stone, never one to miss an opportunity to break tension, sidled up to Gabriella and, with exaggerated flair, began to "bump" dance beside her. "I love retro dancing!" he exclaimed, flashing his trademark grin as the rest laughed. Everyone except Antwan, whose reptilian eyes narrowed with disdain before he turned sharply and stalked off.

Sebastian, always quick to criticize, wasted no time. "Why must the two of you insist on provoking our hosts? Do you think this is a game?" His voice carried an edge of genuine anger this time. The weight of their precarious situation, coupled with the stress of weeks spent in this war zone, was pressing down on him.

Gabriella responded with a cryptic Swedish phrase, "den förrädare, dödlig inget fel mål en drabbning—the snake is deadly no matter which end you encounter." Without waiting for a response, she turned and walked away, leaving the group in uncomfortable silence.

As night fell over the camp, a rare energy buzzed through the air. Even among the makeshift homes of refugees, there was a sense of fleeting joy. Tin cans and scraps were hung up as decorations, and for a brief moment, people pretended being somewhere else—far from the daily horror that surrounded them. The doctors had planned their own small escape, dressing for the occasion.

The older female doctors, faces worn by years of hardship, applied makeup and perfume, trying in vain to mask the ever-present scent of blood and death that seemed permanently embedded in their skin. They giggled like teenagers, transforming themselves, just for a short time, into the people they had been before war had consumed their lives.

"Come on, ladies, we mustn't be late!" called Sebastian, striding past their tent with a stiff formality that clashed with the fraternity blazer he wore—an artifact from his privileged past. The two doctors hurried after him, eager to leave behind the grim reality of the camp.

As they rounded the bend, Gabriella emerged from her tent in a breathtaking display of elegance. Her long, dark hair flowed in waves over her shoulders, catching the light of a single overhead lamp. She wore a short black dress that revealed her long, toned legs, and a pair of Jimmy Choo heels added to her already considerable height. Diamond earrings sparkled in her ears, reflecting the harsh light with a glimmer of defiance.

Sebastian's jaw nearly dropped. "Amazing. Beautiful," he muttered, at once regretting his outburst as the group laughed. Gabriella only smirked, giving him a knowing look before the group made their way down the hill.

At the van, a surly guard checked his clipboard, almost ignoring them. The local Islamic nurse was already inside, wrapped in her parka with a hesitant smile, uncomfortable with the festivities but trying her best to blend in. "Wait—where's Stone?" Gabriella asked, her voice carrying an unintentional hint of anticipation that made the others exchange knowing looks.

As if on cue, Stone came jogging down the hill, dressed in chinos, a sports jacket, and a tie that was a bit askew. "The boy actually knows how to comb his hair?" Sebastian quipped; his surprise was almost unconcealed.

Stone grinned, unflappable as ever. "No worries, mate. It's a clip-on, and I'm not wearing any underwear, in case you're wondering." His words were met with laughter, except for Sebastian, who muttered something about "barbarians" under his breath as he climbed into the van.

Stone held the door for Gabriella, bowing theatrically as she stepped up. He leaned in, inhaling the intoxicating scent of her perfume—an alluring mix of flowers and spice that sent his heart racing. "All dolled up, I see," he whispered, his voice low and teasing.

Gabriella shot him a sultry look, her eyes catching the dim light as she lifted her leg to step into the van, revealing a tantalizing glimpse of her upper thigh. "You clean up pretty well yourself," she replied, her voice a soft purr.

The van sped off into the night, careening through the narrow streets of Beirut as fireworks exploded overhead. The bright bursts of color illuminated the darkened buildings, momentarily blinding the doctors as they peered out the windows. The chaotic energy of the city, coupled with the ever-present threat of violence, created a tense undercurrent, even amid the festivities.

Inside the van, the gravity of the situation fell heavily upon Stone. The night was supposed to be a celebration, a brief escape, but he couldn't shake the feeling that something was about to go terribly wrong. The Colonel's "generosity" felt too easy, too convenient. And as they hurtled toward the unknown, Stone's mind raced with the possibilities—none of them good.

CHAPTER 34

Restaurant Tawlet

The air in Beirut felt thick, not from the heat, but from the tension that hung between the ancient buildings. Two security vans screeched to a halt, spewing out half a dozen men armed with AK-47s. Their dark eyes swept the streets, blocking traffic and forcing a semi-circle perimeter around the group's vehicle. They waved off curious bystanders who gawked at the westerners, their presence stirring unease in the locals. The man in charge, identifiable by the earpiece nestled in his left ear, silently directed the group into the restaurant, his gaze never leaving the rooftops.

"Now this is what I call the red carpet treatment," the American quipped, a smirk pulling at his lips as he held the door open for the women. His Southern drawl, laid-back, did little to conceal the undercurrent of alertness in his posture. Sebastian, in his flamboyant jacket, strode forward, the self-appointed leader of the group, pushing the door open like a king entering his court. The restaurant, Tawlet, embraced them with cool, air-conditioned relief, and the subdued hum of live jazz. It was like stepping into a different era—a place where Beirut's old soul met its modern heartbeat.

The dining room exuded an effortless charm, a blend of rustic simplicity and elegance. Tawlet, nestled in the trendy Mar

Mikhael neighborhood, was famed not just for its food, but for the warmth of its female chef, whom everyone affectionately called "Mom." The tragedy of her story—sons lost to Lebanon's endless wars—was known to all, a testament to the resilience of the Lebanese people. Yet, despite her personal losses, she and her team of female sous-chefs crafted dishes that made the restaurant the culinary pride of the nation.

The table was already heaving under the weight of a banquet: manaqish—flatbreads topped with a fragrant mix of kishka, a fermented and dried yogurt concoction. Beside it, kibbeh nayeh—goat-meat tartare—and h'risset 'akkub, a hearty lamb and wild thistle porridge rarely found on menus. The aroma of fresh herbs, lemon, and the earthy musk of lamb filled the air, competing with the jazz for the diners' attention.

The maître d', a large man with eyes like midnight and a scar that traced a jagged path from his ear to his chin, approached. Moorote, a legend in his own right, once fought alongside great revolutionaries. His loyalty had earned him this establishment, and the respect of everyone from politicians to street urchins. Tonight, however, his demeanor betrayed no hint of his violent past as he guided them through the dining room, past tables of well-dressed businessmen, bodyguards with steely eyes, and women who clung to their men like expensive accessories. Gabriella noticed everything—the way each man had two bodyguards, one watching him, the other scanning the room.

"Do you think the president himself is coming to dinner?" Dr. Stone whispered to her as they walked toward their table. He gestured to the photos on the wall, framed images of Moorote shaking hands with past American presidents.

She smirked, but the unease didn't leave her. There was an overly controlled atmosphere. The guards, the half-hidden guns, the veiled threats in every side glance. Something was off. Yet, as Sebastian waved for champagne, oblivious to the undercurrents of danger, they sat down to enjoy their meal.

CHAPTER 35

The Meal

Laughter and music reverberated through the restaurant, the sound system now pumping out heavy bass beats that overtook the gentle jazz. The group had settled into the festivities, but the undercurrent of tension lingered. Drinks flowed freely, and Sebastian reveled in the attention of two women, hardly noticing the world around him. Stone, however, remained vigilant, indulging in kibbeh nayeh while his instincts sharpened. Something seemed off.

The nurse, who had reluctantly joined the party, sat in silence, sipping her tea. She had resisted the doctors' insistence to stay, but her sense of duty kept her there. As a group of men entered, their voices loud and aggressive, she tensed. Their Arabic slurs were drowned out by the music, but she caught every word, her stomach tightening with fear. She tugged on the French doctor's sleeve.

"Please, we must leave," she urged, her voice scarcely audible over the thumping beat. "It's past curfew."

"Nonsense!" the French doctor shouted back; her face flushed from the wine. "We're fine! Look around. Everyone is having fun."

The nurse's unease grew. She relocated to the end of the table, separating herself from the rowdy group, but her heart froze as three hulking men emerged from the kitchen. They walked past the now frighten guard with a slight glance and stopped in front of her. One leaned down, his breath hot and pungent with the stench of garlic and lamb.

"Sister," he spat, his glazed eyes locking onto hers, "why are you with these people?"

The nurse trembled, her voice just a whisper. "They are good doctors... they help the children..."

His hand lashed out, silencing her with a dismissive gesture. He straightened up, towering over her like a predator. "They're the reason this war never ends. Those refugees... should be dead."

At the bar, Stone had already clocked the men. Something primal stirred in him—a warning deep in his gut. He recognized the type: dangerous, ruthless. These men remain on the radar of every intelligence agency from Washington to Tel Aviv. They backed the Lebanese military and direct competition with the party's host. How they roamed so freely out in the open no one knew. These high-ranking operatives who operated in the shadows, untouchable by law, but not by Stone.

His eyes flicked to Gabriella, her lithe form swaying to the beat, her eyes half-lidded but scanning the room, always alert. She moved like a predator, her instincts as keen as his. She had already noticed the men. Stone pushed himself away from the bar, feigning drunkenness as he made his way toward the restroom, his body loose, unthreatening. But his thoughts were racing, calculating his next move.

Across the room, the leader of the trio grabbed a fistful of the French doctor's hair, yanking her head back as she screamed.

Chaos erupted. Gabriella sprinted across the floor, her movements fluid and controlled. The maître d', Moorote, rushed toward the men, pleading for peace, but his words were cut short as the leader unsheathed a massive janbia, plunging it into Moorote's throat. Blood sprayed in an arc, drenching the diners closest to the altercation. Gabriella wasted no time. She lunged, using the man's momentary arrogance against him.

In a flash, she drove her knee into his groin, followed by a vicious strike to his throat. He gasped, his eyes wide with disbelief as she delivered a final blow using a spear hand strike with her index figure reinforced by her middle, together forming a force greater than a punch entered his eye, incapacitating him. Stone was on the second bodyguard before anyone could react, wrapping his arm around the man's neck in a tight chokehold followed by a vicious twist jerking his head upward. It was quick, efficient. The body went limp and fell to the ground.

The fight was over in seconds, but the aftermath hung in the air like a dark cloud. The maître d' lay dying, The doctors rushed to his aid, the team worked desperately to save him knowing it was futile. Gabriella and Stone, soaked in crimson, stood over the bodies.

"We need to leave," Stone growled, wiping blood from his face.

"We can't just abandon him!" Sebastian shouted, his hands futilely pressing against the maître d's gushing wound.

"There's nothing more we can do for him," Gabriella snapped, her voice cold. "Look around. The guards are gone. We're on our own."

They staggered out into the deserted street, the celebratory noise of the New Year fading into the background. Beirut had become a ghost town. The vans vanished, and their lone option was to make the perilous journey back to camp on foot.

With danger lurking in every shadow, they moved like hunted animals, slipping through the alleyways as military vehicles patrolled the streets. By the time they reached the safety of camp, they were exhausted, bloodied, and forever changed. Stone realized this marked only the start. Something far darker lay ahead.

CHAPTER 36

Camp

Gabriella slipped into her tent, peeling off the sweat-soaked dress from her body with swift efficiency. She rummaged through her rucksack, finding a pair of lightweight shorts and a tank top, her hands moving with purpose as the night air clung to her skin. Tossing aside her underwear, she wrapped herself in a towel, grabbed her Toms, and headed for the shower tent, eyes scanning the deserted camp. No one around.

Inside his own tent, Stone's movements were those of someone very comfortable working under duress. He moved with practiced precision. His gear slid into the duffle bag, the clothes from tonight's operation stuffed into the corner of a nearby dumpster with a flick of his wrist. He moved toward the shower tent, dressed only in boxers, his bare feet undisturbed by the rough terrain. A low whistle escaped his lips, the tune casual, masking the adrenaline still coursing through his veins. He caught a glimpse of a familiar silhouette ahead. Gabriella. He grinned, the corner of his mouth lifting as the image of her confident stride slipped into the darkness of the tent.

The shower tent stood at the edge of the camp, hastily constructed but functional, the poles straining under the weight of the 400-liter water drum. The setup was crude, two shower compartments divided by a thin, transparent curtain. Privacy was a suggestion, not a guarantee. The drum, now heated by the extensive day's sun, offered a brief respite of lukewarm water before the chill would inevitably set in.

Stone pulled back the tent flap just as Gabriella stepped under the water. He had heard her footsteps before, the crunch of gravel beneath her shoes too familiar to mistake. His smile deepened. Was she amused; he wondered? Or simply aware of the game they were playing? He had killed a man hours ago, yet here he was, bare-chested and humming. The military left its mark in strange ways. Gabriella surely sensed it. She always seemed to see more than she let on.

"You seem to be in good spirits," she called out, her voice teasing as she pulled the curtain tight around her body. She peeked out, eyes glinting in the low light as they settled on his boxer shorts, the absurd dolphin pattern eliciting a smirk.

Stone raised an eyebrow. "Oh, hey there. Didn't notice anyone else was around."

"Didn't notice the light?" she teased, voice soft yet sharp.

Stone shrugged, his grin widening. "Nah, just watching my step." His green eyes met hers, sparkling with mischief and something else—an invitation. A flicker of something passed between them, a magnetic pull in the humid air.

Gabriella's gaze lingered longer than intended, tracing the hard lines of his chest, the sculpted muscles that flexed effortlessly with each movement. His body was better than just fit—it was a map of endurance, resilience, each scar telling its own story. Her face flushed as she realized how intently she'd been staring. She turned away, her heart pounding with something unfamiliar, something she hadn't felt in a long time.

Stone chuckled, the sound low and warm, catching her in the act. He knew the effect his physique had on people—strangers asking about his workout routine or how much he could bench—but it was the scars that truly marked him, the reminders of battles fought and survived.

"You were incredible tonight," he said, changing the subject with practiced ease. "The way you jumped in to protect your friends—that was something."

Gabriella didn't respond straight away. Instead, her mind raced. Stone wasn't just a doctor—there was more to him. She had seen men like him before, ones with pasts they kept buried under layers of charm and nonchalance. Her instincts told her there was danger beneath his easygoing exterior, and she wasn't sure if that excited or terrified her.

Without warning, Stone dropped his shorts, the motion smooth and deliberate. He kicked them onto the wooden bench by her towel and underwear, the sudden shift catching her off guard. He tossed his towel atop the pile and walked into the adjacent stall, the curtain doing little to hide the solid lines of his body.

Gabriella swallowed hard; her throat dry. She turned the water on, letting it cascade over her, masking the heat rising in her chest that had nothing to do with the lukewarm water. Her thoughts scrambled for clarity, but Stone's voice cut through the fog.

"You were saying something?" he asked, his voice low, stepping closer, his presence undeniable even through the thin curtain. His hand reached around her, offering the bar of soap, his body brushing against hers in the confined space. The contact was electric. His strength was palpable to her, the controlled power that hummed just beneath the surface.

Gabriella fumbled for words, her pulse racing. She dropped the soap, bending to retrieve it, but before she reacted, Stone closed the distance between them. His hands gripped her waist, firm and unyielding. She gasped, the sound escaping her lips before she could stifle it. Their bodies in sync, a rhythm of need and release, the tension that had built between them over the past couple of days erupting in the small confines of the tent.

A primal urge propelled their hurried movements, an irresistible force for both. The water had long since turned cold, but neither of them noticed. The sound of their bodies, the slick heat of the moment, drowned out everything else.

When they emerged, towels wrapped hastily around their bodies, the tent was askew, the poles leaning precariously. Gabriella caught Stone's eye, a knowing smile passing between them as they slipped out into the night, hand in hand.

But they weren't alone.

Sebastian, still groggy from his earlier drunken stupor, stumbled toward the makeshift urinals, his bleary eyes catching sight of the two figures darting toward Gabriella's tent, their bodies, glistening and almost naked. He squinted, piecing together what he had seen.

CHAPTER 37

Morning

The camp awoke to chaos, as the thunderous boom of artillery shells shattered the early morning stillness. Dust and debris kicked up around the camp's perimeter, enveloping the landscape in a veil of sand. Panic spread like wildfire as shrieks and cries erupted from women and children, their voices almost drowned out by the increasingly loud explosions. Buildings trembled, tents collapsed, and a wave of desperate refugees surged forward, trampling everything and everyone in their path.

Inside her tent, Gabriella and Stone were jolted awake, tumbling out of their cot. The air was thick with the acrid scent of smoke. Scrambling for their clothes, they scarcely had time to react when an Arab coordinator burst in, eyes wide with fear, his face ashen. "Please help! They come, they come now!"

Gabriella tried to calm him, but the terror in his eyes rendered him incoherent. "No, no, not good, everyone dies," he stammered, his broken English more frantic than usual.

Stone moved toward him, his calm demeanor a stark contrast to the panic around them. He placed a firm hand on the man's shoulder. "Tell us what's going on."

The man pointed north, where a plume of smoke twisted into the sky. His shaking hand then gestured west, where thick, gray clouds loomed like an ominous shroud, blotting out the early morning sun. "Bad man died last night in the city. Now...everyone dies."

The cryptic warning sent a shiver through Gabriella as she watched the man dash off, joining the stampede of refugees fleeing toward the camp's eastern edge.

"We need to move," Stone said, his voice steady but laced with urgency. Gabriella nodded, grabbing her backpack as Stone sprinted toward his tent on the west side, the area closest to the shelling. "I'll meet you at the surgery," he called over his shoulder, disappearing into the chaos before she could protest.

Stone reached his tent, now a tangle of burning debris. Thick black smoke billowed from craters where tents and supplies had once stood. The fence along the western side of the camp was now engulfed in flames, cutting off any escape route. He ducked under the smoldering remains of his tent and pulled out his duffle bag. Relieved, he found his father's wristwatch intact and stuffed it into his pocket.

As he went to leave, something in the corner of his vision caught his attention—a small, charred limb protruding from the debris. Stone's heart clenched. Without hesitation, he sprinted toward the rubble and kicked away the burning boards, revealing a young boy, no older than ten, one leg missing. The child's body was almost un-recognizable beneath the burns, but Stone recognized him—a patient from the previous day's surgery.

Stone checked for a pulse. Faint, but there. He scooped the boy into his arms, his body shockingly light. An explosion nearby sent a shockwave of debris raining down as Stone ran toward the surgery tent, weaving through the panicked crowd, his eyes scanning for threats. The boy's faint breath seemed to quicken with each step, each second slipping away.

Inside the surgery tent, chaos reigned. Two female doctors hastily packing supplies, their faces etched with fear. Operating tables had been broken down, plastic-wrapped and stacked on carts. Vital machines similarly packed, ready for transport. Stone stood in shock, his voice rising above the din. "What the hell is going on?"

Sebastian strolled in, unbothered by the carnage outside, still wearing his jacket from the night before. "We're evacuating, chum. Haven't you heard the bombs?" His tone dripped with condescension, his smirk a cruel mockery of the chaos around them.

"This boy needs attention—now!" Stone barked, his patience fraying.

Before any response, Colonel Hajj Multicki appeared at the tent's entrance, his eyes cold, his demeanor commanding. "All die someday," he commented in broken English, his voice eerily calm amidst the terror.

Stone, still holding the boy, turned toward Sebastian, his frustration boiling over. "Why the rush? Why is everything packed? Who ordered this?"

Sebastian didn't answer, humming a classical tune as he stuffed surgical tools into his old-fashioned doctor's bag, his indifference stoking Stone's rage.

Before Stone could react, the Colonel walked forward, pulled out a revolver, and without hesitation, shot the boy in the head. The tent fell into stunned silence, the sound of the shot still ringing in their ears as blood splattered across their faces. Stone stood frozen, his grip slackening as the lifeless body slid from his arms to the ground.

"We go now," the Colonel said, his gun still trained on Stone. Armed men poured into the tent; their rifles aimed at the doctors. Gabriella, shaken but resolute, placed a hand on Stone's shoulder, a silent plea for restraint.

"We have to move," Gabriella urged, her voice trembling with fear. "Eastern side, now."

They just made it ten meters when a deafening explosion ripped through the camp. The ground shook violently as a wave of heat and debris engulfed them. Stone and Gabriella were thrown to the ground, landing hard amidst the wreckage of collapsed tents and burning refuse.

Gabriella cried out in pain, clutching her leg. Blood pooled around her shoe; a shard of shrapnel embedded deep in her calf. Stone acted quickly, tying a tourniquet just below her knee, his hands moving with the practiced precision of a man who had seen plenty of war's cruelty.

"Can you walk?" he asked, his voice gentle but firm. Gabriella nodded, though her face was pale, her breath labored. He hoisted her onto her feet, supporting her weight as they limped from the burning wreckage, the air thick with the acrid stench of smoke and blood.

Behind them, the camp was a smoldering ruin, a hellish landscape of flames, bodies, and shattered lives. Stone glanced once over his shoulder, seeing the crater where Sebastian and the vehicles had stood moments before. Nothing remained but twisted metal and scorched earth.

CHAPTER 38

Eastern Exit

The scene was chaos. Hundreds of refugees surged through the shattered gate, their footsteps grinding it into the sand as they fled toward the sea. The relentless pounding of artillery had stopped for now, but the distant rumble of explosions still echoed in their ears. Overhead, the sky was a burnt orange haze, the sun smothered by the smoke of burning buildings. The salty tang of the ocean was faint, cutting through the stench of sweat, blood, and fear.

Stone's muscles ached as he helped Gabriella limp along, her weight pressing into his side. Her leg, now bandaged but still bleeding, left dark spots in the dust with every step. They'd walked a few kilometers when he spotted an abandoned building—a scorched husk of cement and steel, riddled with bullet holes. It was as good a place as any to stop.

"Sit here," Stone instructed, easing Gabriella down onto a crumbling doorstep. The air felt heavier near the shoreline, tinged with the threat of increased violence. He scanned the horizon. Refugees still flooded toward the distant UN ships; a beacon of safety they weren't sure even existed anymore.

Gabriella leaned back against the wall, her face pale, her breath ragged. "Are you really going to do this here?" she asked, her voice strained.

Stone pulled out a first-aid kit, suited for survival than precision. "What better spot for surgery than a seaside ruin?" he replied, forcing a smile. His heart pounded, but he couldn't let her see it. Not now.

Her laugh was brittle. "Great bedside manner, doc."

As Stone positioned her leg, he caught the metallic scent of blood mixed with dirt and God knows what else. The wound was deep, and the shrapnel sticking out was worse than he'd feared—jagged, dirty, and dangerous. He poured alcohol over it without warning.

"Goddammit, Stone!" Gabriella shrieked, grabbing her leg in agony.

"Sorry," Stone muttered, his focus intense. He threaded the needle with practiced precision, his hands steady despite the adrenaline coursing through him.

"You couldn't have warned me?" she snapped, her face contorted in pain.

He glanced up, smirking. "Wouldn't have helped. Now stop complaining. I'm thinking of signing my masterpiece."

She winced but managed a weak grin. "Hilarious," she grumbled through clenched teeth.

Stone tightened the tourniquet higher up her thigh. His eyes darkened as he pulled the jagged piece of shrapnel free with a swift yank. It was larger than either of them had expected. Blood spurted from the wound, but Stone quickly applied pressure, his hands moving with surgical efficiency. He on just noticed the refugees stumbling past them, lost in their own world of fear and exhaustion.

Gabriella's skin grew paler. Stone's voice cut through her fog. "Before you pass out, I have a question." His tone was casual, too casual.

"Shut up," she muttered, her voice weak.

He injected Lidocaine into her calf, buying them both sometime before the pain returned. As he worked, his mind raced, piecing together the puzzle that had haunted him since they'd fled the camp. His hands moved with precision, stitching her wound, but his thoughts were on something else.

"You put something in Sebastian's pocket," not looking up from his work.

Gabriella's head snapped up, her eyes narrowing. "What?"

"I saw it," Stone continued, his voice low. "When you hugged him. Subtle, but I caught it. A tracking device, correct?"

She sighed, her body slumping against the wall. "You got me."

"Figured as much," tying off the final stitch. "You practically shoved us out of the camp as soon as Sebastian left. Then boom—explosion."

The silence between them grew, filled with the unspoken tension of the moment. Gabriella flexed her leg gingerly, testing the stitches. The wound was sealed, but the ache was deep. Stone stood, brushing the blood and dust from his hands.

"Some of my best work," though his voice lacked its usual humor. He watched her, waiting for her to say something, anything to explain what was going on.

Gabriella stood slowly, leaning on him for balance. Her eyes met his, and for a moment, the weight of everything unsaid hung between them. Then, without warning, she kissed him. It was brief, intense, and left Stone momentarily stunned. She pulled away, limping toward the port.

"You faker!" he called after her, rushing to catch up.

Gabriella smirked over her shoulder, but her eyes were clouded with something darker, something haunted. "Fine, I'll take the Vicodin," she said, snatching the pill from his hand before he poped it into his mouth.

She paused for a moment, looking into his eyes, her voice dropping to a whisper. "I'll tell you everything."

Stone's heart skipped a beat. This was it—the truth. Even as he walked beside her, a gnawing feeling of dread took hold. Whatever she had to reveal, it wasn't just about a tracking device. This was deeper, more dangerous than either of them had anticipated.

And as the sea breeze brushed past them, carrying the distant echo of additional artillery, Stone knew they were far from out of the storm.

CHAPTER 39

The Port of Beirut

The air reeked of sweat, salt, and smoke, a cocktail of desperation as refugees flooded the docks, trampling the gate underfoot the frantic rush towards the UN ships resembled a final, desperate attempt to survive. Shelling had ceased, but the ominous thump of artillery could still be felt, a distant pulse of the war raging behind them. Stone's arm tightened around Gabriella's waist, helping her limp toward the dock. Her leg, hastily bandaged, left a thin trail of blood, staining the dust at their feet.

Stone's eyes swept over the swarm of desperate people. His UN-affiliated medical badge caught the attention of a guard, and with a quick flash of credentials, they were waved through. Inside the perimeter, the atmosphere was marginally calmer, but tension lingered in the air like static before a storm. They were escorted to the medical area, where Gabriella was treated by a harried Indian doctor. He acknowledged their presence once he discovered they were professionals, only stopping to ask if they could assist later, before hurrying on to another patient.

Stone's gaze flicked to Gabriella. She remained silent, her face pale as the doctor applied fresh bandages and gave her a tetanus shot. She winced but said nothing, her thoughts clearly elsewhere.

Upon receiving clearance, they proceeded to a cabin

adjacent to the captain's quarters. The door marked "2B." Stone couldn't help but quip, "To be or not to be, that is the question." His attempt at levity earned him a groan from Gabriella, who pushed open the door and collapsed onto the lower bunk. Within seconds, she was out cold.

Stone stood in the doorway, surveying the room. It was small but secure. He closed the door with a low click, his senses still on high alert. He needed to get the lay of the ship, to understand its movements and its people. Locking the door behind him, he set off down the narrow corridor toward the bridge.

As soon as he left, Gabriella's eyes snapped open. She sat up with caution, wincing as the pain in her leg throbbed in rhythm with her heartbeat. She reached for her bag, the weight of what she carried heavier than the actual object. The UN guards hadn't bothered to search them thoroughly—after all, they were medics. How easy it was to smuggle contraband through official channels, she thought wryly.

Pulling out her compact mirror, she examined herself. Her face looked gaunt, hollowed out by exhaustion. "God, I look awful," she muttered. Then, with a flick, she pressed the hidden latch inside the mirror. A faint ping sounded from the concealed homing device. Now she waited. It might take hours, but the signal was out. Leaning back against the pillow, she closed her eyes, her mind racing over how much she could afford to tell Stone. The extent of his suspicions.

CHAPTER 40

The Dockside

Stone approached the bridge, but the language barrier was thick. The men on board had limited English skills, nor Arabic, and his attempts to engage them were met with indifferent shrugs. They gestured vaguely toward the starboard side, and Stone took the hint, heading down to the lower decks.

At the dockside, the scene was grim. UN guards, overwhelmed by the crush of humanity, had closed the gates to the ship. Desperate refugees clung to the chain-link fence, their hands reaching through the gaps as the guards tossed blankets and bags of rice over the top. Fights broke out for the scarce supplies. Stone clenched his jaw, unable to watch the chaos any longer.

He turned his gaze inland. Dark plumes of smoke rose from the hillside where the camp had been. The shelling had lessened, but the sight of those smoke trails stretched a kilometer in length gnawed at him. It wasn't over—whatever was happening, it marked the beginning.

Looking out to sea, Stone scanned the horizon. A handful of UN vessels floated nearby, cargo and support ships, mostly. No destroyers in sight. He silently cursed. If only there were artillery, something to strike back at the bastards bombarding the camp. But not today. There was no oil or lucrative resource here, nothing to attract the attention of a bigger military force. Just people, and people didn't matter in the grand geopolitical game.

His eyes caught sight of a frigate in the distance. It was hard to make out the flag, but Stone had a hunch. Israel. They patrolled these waters with an iron fist, watching over Lebanon's southern coast. He glanced down at his watch, feeling the weight of time pressing in on him. He had to move fast. The game was changing, and Gabriella was in the center of it.

Stone returned to their cabin with a tray of flatbread and tangerines. He slipped in, not wanting to disturb Gabriella, who was still asleep, or at least pretending to be. The cabin was dark, soundproof, offering a rare moment of peace in the middle of chaos. He set the food down beside her, then sank into the lone chair by the bunk.

For the first time in hours, Stone allowed himself to pause, to breathe. His body ached from tension, the constant adrenaline leaving his muscles trembling. He pulled a little tin from his bag, popping a blue Xanax and a white Vicodin into his mouth. The bitter taste of the pills made him grimace. He never could swallow pills like a normal person.

As the drugs kicked in, Stone stretched out on the opposite bunk, slowing his heart rate with deep breaths. He knew he had to stay sharp, but right now, his body was shutting down, demanding rest. Within minutes, sleep claimed him.

Hours later, Stone woke to Gabriella's steady breathing, her presence warming the small cabin. He didn't open his eyes, instead focusing on the rhythm of her breath, the subtle shift of air between them. His instincts, honed from years in the field, told him she was awake.

Gabriella's leg throbbed as she stood, wincing with each step toward her bag. She peeled off her dirty shorts, muttering under her breath about how she was starting to act like Stone. His deep voice startled her. "Now that's a view I could wake up to every day."

"Men," she huffed, flipping her hair over her shoulder. "Always about sex." But she flashed him a devilish smile as she pulled on a sundress, the last clean clothing left in her bag.

Stone sat up, stretching his arms behind his head, his eyes lingering on her. "You know what they say—sex is like pizza."

Gabriella rolled her eyes. "Let me guess, some stupid American saying?"

Stone laughed, standing and pulling on his shorts. "You'd appreciate the meaning. Because you're not who you say you are, are you?"

Gabriella froze, her back to him. Slowly, she turned, her face serious now. "I'm Mossad."

Her confession hung in the air like a challenge, her eyes searching his face for a reaction.

Stone's grin didn't falter. "I figured."

She sighed and gave a faint smile and pulled her hair back into a ponytail. "What about you? CIA? NSA? Military? I saw how you killed that man, that wasn't some random act of bravery or copying moves from some action movie."

Before Gabriella could press him, a knock pounded at the door. Stone's body tensed. The knock came again, louder, followed by a voice shouting for them to open.

They exchanged a glance, both knowing their luck had just shifted. And the stakes were about to get a great deal higher.

Stone stood to his full height, towering in the dim light as he approached the door. He swung it open with a forceful motion, the creak of metal hinges echoing down the narrow corridor. The three men outside took an instinctive step back. Their nervous eyes darted from Stone's muscled frame to his piercing green eyes, which held a sharp intensity that seemed to bore through them.

"What?" Stone's voice was low, controlled, but the undercurrent of menace was clear. His arms folded across his chest, his muscles tightening into an imposing display of strength. The first officer, a thin, jittery man, swallowed hard, his confidence wavering under the Westerner's intimidating presence.

"The captain… he wants you off the ship. Now," the officer stammered, regretting the task he had been given. He glanced nervously at the two junior officers behind him, wishing there were armed guards beside him instead.

"Does he now?" Stone's voice rumbled, his eyes narrowing as he held his ground. He loomed in the doorway, blocking their view of the cabin. Behind him, Gabriella had already slipped on her shoes and shouldered her bag, her movements quick and efficient, betraying no trace of the pain from her injured leg.

"The Bridge. Captain is on the Bridge," the officer stuttered, pointing shakily toward the stairs. He took an extra step back, desperately hoping to distance himself from the confrontation. Stone didn't move, his mind working rapidly, calculating his next move.

He felt Gabriella's hand on his back, her voice soft and

urgent, "I have a ride. We need to leave now, before they get suspicious. It's dark, we'll have cover."

Stone weighed his options, his instincts screaming that something was wrong. Why would the captain want them gone after they had provided medical aid earlier in the day? It didn't add up. But Gabriella's words pulled at his thoughts—if she had an exit strategy, it was time to act.

"Tell your Captain we'll be up shortly." With that, Stone stepped back inside the room, slamming the door in the officer's face. His pulse quickened as he turned to Gabriella, his eyes scanning her face for any hint of deceit. "What do you mean, a ride? Where to? And who exactly are we meeting?"

Gabriella's eyes flashed with frustration, but she held his gaze, her voice steady. "We can't stay here. They know something. Trust me, I have a way out, but we need to move fast."

Stone didn't like the vagueness in her answer. His gut told him there was more she wasn't saying. Still, she had been right before. "Fine," he muttered. "But I want answers."

Gabriella nodded curtly, her eyes softening. "You'll get them. But first, we survive."

Without a further word, they headed down toward the lower decks, slipping through the shadows cast by the towering crates of grain and supplies being loaded and unloaded around the clock. The clang of metal and the rumble of forklifts filled the air as they passed swiftly, unnoticed in the chaos.

The scene outside the gates was far worse. Refugees clawed at the fences, their faces gaunt and desperate, hands outstretched for any scraps of food tossed from above. Guards, overwhelmed and indifferent, ignored the cries for help, while many took bribes, tossing half-hearted rations to those who could pay. Stone clenched his jaw, fury bubbling beneath the surface. "What good are cans of pears without can openers?" he muttered, disgusted.

Gabriella sighed; her voice resigned. "It's always been like this. The strong prey on the weak, and the cycle never ends."

Stone glanced at her, feeling the weight of her words as they neared the fence. His muscles tense with frustration. They stopped at the gate, the guards hardly stirring from their resting places. Stone pulled out his SWMP2 folding combat knife, a flash of steel catching the dim light. Gabriella's eyes widened, scanning the ship's upper decks for any signs of movement as Stone plunged the blade into the cans, twisting off the tops with ease. He handed them to the children on the opposite side of the fence, their eyes wide with disbelief before they darted away with their prize.

"Let's go," Stone growled, pressing his massive frame against the fence, bending the metal with his strength to create a gap just wide enough for them to slip through. Gabriella moved forward, her injured leg making her wince as she ducked under his arm. She shot him with a teasing glance, her hip brushing against him. "Sorry, bag's a bit big."

Stone smirked. "Yeah, sure. And women say men are shallow?"

Once through the fence, they kept close to the shadows, moving along the perimeter at a brisk pace. Gabriella limped, but her resolve was iron. By the fishing boats, moored for the night, they made a brief stop, the water gently lapping against the hulls.

Stone's eyes scanned the horizon. "Let me check that leg."

Gabriella shook her head, pointing to the open sea. "No time. We have to get out there. They'll pick us up near the breaker."

Stone's eyes narrowed. "Who are they?"

Before Gabriella could answer, a loud crack echoed through the night. The side of the boat splintered as a bullet struck inches from Stone's head. Instinct kicked in, and they both dropped to the sand, their bodies pressed flat against the cool ground as another shot rang out, the water splashing up around them.

"Move!" Stone hissed, pulling Gabriella forward as they crawled toward the cover of the boat. Her breath came in quick, shallow bursts, her heart racing with the tension of the moment.

Stone's mind raced; every sense heightened. Whoever was shooting knew they were there—but how? And why? This wasn't random, and he was certain now that Gabriella's 'ride' wasn't just a lucky escape. She was hiding something from him.

CHAPTER 41

Young Jabil

Jabil received the call late in the evening. The targets were confirmed, and time was of the essence. The promise of a bonus spurred him into action, his MPx4 dirt bike already waiting at the bottom of his flat's stairs. Despite the neighbors complaining among themselves, but never to him. Jabil belonged to a militia since he was fourteen—a survival mechanism in a city where violence ruled the streets and allegiances were more potent than religion. Muslim or Christian, it didn't matter. On any given day, a man may be beaten, robbed, or killed for no reason at all.

Joining a gang was his only recourse. Strength in numbers, they said. The streets didn't forgive the weak, and Jabil had rapidly risen through the ranks. His reputation for recklessness—Akhwat, they called him, meaning "crazy"—preceded him. He wasn't afraid to do what everyone else wouldn't. It was that fearlessness, the willingness to go further, that had marked his ascension.

The memory of his first kill lingered. He and his friends were caught by police stealing from a fruit vendor. Most of his companions fled, but not Jabil. He stood his ground, beaten mercilessly. The bruises sent a public message: This is what happens to thieves. He had been left in the street like a broken doll, and not a soul came to his aid. Even his neighbors kept their distance, afraid to get involved.

The proceeding day, Jabil returned to the same street. The bruises remain fresh, the pain sharp, but his resolve was harder. A blunt, old butcher's knife from his family's kitchen was his only companion. He found the policemen laughing, relaxed, their backs to the street outside a pastry shop. For Jabil, this would be too easy, he stole from tourists and locals alike by sneaking up on them without being detected. This time he steal a life. There was no mistaking the policeman who had beaten him from an inch of his life for he had the largest neck and round obese body among them. His eyes locked onto the biggest of the group—Anta Samini, fatty. They called him who couldn't even reach his own sidearm without effort. Jabil was seeing red, driven by revenge.

Jabil walked within two storefronts with his weapon of choice by his side. He stopped as an expensive-looking car with tinted windows pulled up to the group of policemen. The two passengers side windows rolled down and Jabil saw two automatic weapons sticking out before the world irrupted with gunfire and screaming people as the Policemen fell like dominos, their bodies jerking as bullets tore through them. Except for anta Samini, he was left unharmed. He stood frozen, sweat pouring down his oversized face, his eyes wide with terror. Jabil kept walking, undeterred by the carnage. He was close now— a short distance from Samini. The butcher's knife in his hand felt heavier than ever, and the urge to kill pulsated through him.

The rear door opened and well-dressed man stepped out holding, an automatic weapon in one hand. Sunglasses obscuring his face, long wavy hair past his shoulders and dressed in the latest European suite, down to the expensive loafers. Jabil speculated that the individual was Arab but remained unsure about their place of origin.

The man saw Jabil's knife and smirked, pointing at him with his gun. "Are you here to protect him?" His voice was calm, gesturing with his left thumb jerked back at the policeman, too shocked to move.

Jabil didn't flinch. "I came to kill him," he shouted, more for Samini's benefit than the stranger's.

"Why?" the man asked.

Jabil lifted his shirt, revealing the fresh bruises and broken bones. "Because of this."

The man studied Jabil; his expression unreadable behind the dark glasses. "Did you deserve it?" he asked, lowering his weapon to some degree.

Jabil hesitated. He could lie, but something about this man made him pause. "Yes," he admitted. "I was stealing, but... I was protecting the vendor from worse thieves."

A grin spread across the man's face, and laughter echoed from the car behind him. "So, you're an enforcer of sorts?" Looks like you didn't do a great job." The man's tone was casual, but his words cut deep.

The man handed Jabil the weapon, stepping back. Jabil stared at the gun, knowing this was no random act of trust. It was a test. He had the chance to kill the man instantly. He could have dropped the weapon and runaway and become a fisherman like his distant family male members has done before him, or so he thought he remembered being told such stories. Something stopped him, instead, Jabil did what he had come to do.

He walked around the stranger and aimed the weapon at Samini. The cop's fat fingers fumbled for his gun; it was already too late. The automatic weapon bucked in Jabil's hands, the sound of the gunfire deafening. Samini dropped, his body a lifeless heap on the blood-soaked pavement.

Laughter erupted again from the car. The man advanced, holding out his hand. "Little brother, can I have my gun back?" Jabil handed it over, numb with the weight of what he had done. The man's words echoed in his head: Come with us, and you'll be free. Rich, even.

Jabil had slid into the back seat of the car, his future decided in that moment. He became a killer, taking lives as easily as others took a breath. Men, women, children—it didn't matter. The job was the job.

Years later, the thrill was gone. The bloodlust, once intoxicating, had dulled. Killing was now a clinical act, a necessity rather than a pleasure. Jabil had perfected his craft, learning to keep his distance from his targets, to avoid the emotional rush that once drove him. His employers needed him sharp, invisible. Any mistake would compromise the entire organization.

New Years Eve

Since it was the start of the new year, he decided to go to the upscale restaurant where all the international elites would gather. He didn't need an invitation. He had taken care of a problem for the owner, someone extorting him. He likens it to the wild west, he thought many times as he watched the movie Tombstone and Wyatt Earp, firing his guns with both hands. He couldn't connect that them being law enforcers, unlike him, a cold-hearted hired killer.

He came alone, dressed up in his favorite American sports jack, hand tailored with extra-long pocket on the left side. It was sewn at an angle and reinforced double snitching, which at the time the tailor had not understood why the young man requested such an odd request. The pocket was deeper than most and narrower at the bottom.

Jambil slid a Glock into the pocket with a silencer screwed on. Beamed at himself in the mirror. No one would notice if he had a weapon unless he was searched at the door.

Jambil had come closer to 1130pm, knowing the party be warming up to his likening. He looked up space at the packed bar and ordered a martini. Acting as a secret agent in his mind for his own amusement. Observing the crowd unaware of his existence through the expansive mirror above the bar.

There were many important traders of goods and services present from jobbers supplying food and tobacco runs from the sea to the Syrian border guards. Services included human trafficking, weapon dealers alike. All of them each with their own bodyguards. He knew none could prevent him from eliminating anyone of them. He listened to live jazz and admiration for the players this evening. He considered learning to play an instrument, maybe a saxophone he thought. Then again, his instrument was in the special pocket and when it sang, no one danced. Tonight, however, was different.

He was getting into the music, relaxing being louder and extra people dancing. Leaning back taking in all the women around when he notices a disruption in the flow of the party. Out of his periphery three men walking in from the kitchen area. Jambil scanned the exits without turning his head searching for signs of intent aggression in the room. Looking for a likely mark but none that obvious to him with many well contented and wealthy people gathered. It started to look like an interesting night as he took an additional sip of liquor.

Jambil heard rather than saw in the crowded room a loud argument breakout at the extended table. Well-dressed westerners are accosted by the recent guest from the kitchen. While sipping his drink with his left hand, he unbuttoned his jacket with his right. Slid his hand into his favorite pocket and gripped his weapon enjoying the comfort of the handle it brought him. Resting and waiting to be called upon by its master.

Jambil and party goers in the room stopped when the shouting became aggressive, and the restaurant maitre d came to resolve the il behave manners of both parties.

Scuffing began among the guests, bodyguards in the room acted professionally getting closer to their employers and reaching into their own jackets. Jambil noting to himself none of them stood to block protecting their assets, they acted in their own self-interest.

In the sea of bodies, the agitator from the three men pulled a dagger and thrust into the maitr d. Jambil became memorized among the act of violence and people running away a beautiful fit woman with cheetah like moves sprang lunging across the dance floor at the attacker. Moving with greater speed using her body as a true combatant a trained eye could see. Jambil excited took a few steps forward brushing past screaming guest trying to leave the mayhem, halting when the larger man was picked off his feet with a shocked look on his face with a muscular arm encircled his throat.

The woman no longer held the element of surprise, and the two bodyguards drew their weapons on her.

Jambil freed his own gun with a smooth well practice draw placing two precise bullets dead center in each man. His silent bullets found their intended targets plugging into the hearts. The entire restaurant guests, including staff burst for all the exits with bodies lying staining the wood floors of blood. Jambil reacted with emotion, something he had not done in a long time. It must have been the influence of the alcohol he thought as he slides his gun back into its holding pocket still hot from use and he spun around and fled in the crowd of people into the street.

CHAPTER 42

The Beach

Jambil received the call and the descriptions, the source was the Filipino captain from the UN ship himself on their payroll. The captain enjoyed the Lebanese's hospitality and was a rich man from the illegal trading of UN goods supposed to go to the starving, war-torn community instead sold on the black market. The captain described the same couple Jambil had seen the night before at the restaurant. He could pick her out of a sandstorm he thought.

Jambil knew the port well, every kid played at the docks growing up watching the gigantic ships come and go. The elevation he selected had to be above the ship to get a clear shot and view all the possible escape routes. There wasn't much fun knowing exactly when your prey was coming out. The new targets were high-profile: two UN workers who were more than what they seemed. Spies or assassins—Jabil didn't care which. What mattered was that they had killed a powerful man, someone important to his employers. The task of eliminating them had now fallen to Jabil.

He found his vantage point in an old, dilapidated building overlooking the docks. The woman who answered the door hadn't stood a chance. One clean shot under her chin, and she was gone. Jabil barely registered her death as he set up his sniper

Russian IzmashSV-98 rifle on the balcony. The ship would arrive soon, and with it, his targets.

The irony was not lost on him. He had saved the woman's life once, and now he would take it. Through the scope of his rifle, he imagined the moment—her shock, the confusion in her eyes as the initial bullet tore through her companion's head. Then her. He would savor her fear, even if only for a second.

Jabil took a deep breath, the smell of lamb stew still lingering from the old woman's kitchen. He steadied his aim. The night was quiet, the city below him dark and indifferent.

Gabriella's heart pounded like a war drum, adrenaline surging through her veins. How many times a day could someone try to kill her? Stone lay atop her, his body taut, shielding her from the next barrage of bullets. The night was alive with distant gunfire, the hiss of the ocean mingling with the sharp crack of shots.

It would be better if they'd left under the cover of darkness, she thought. The night's gloom being their ally. Stone, sensing her restlessness by the rapid pace of her breathing, pushed himself up. His body held steady in a modified plank position, his muscles trembling under the strain, but his eyes focused like a predator in the night.

"Now's really not the time for a workout, Stone," Gabriella muttered, shifting beneath him. She edged backward, seeking the comfort of the warm water lapping at her skin. It brought with it a flood of memories—her home, the nearby beach. She clung to the hope that she would return there. Not tonight, not here, she told herself.

"There's always time for exercise," Stone whispered, that infuriating grin flashing across his face, even amidst the chaos.

Gabriella snorted. "You think you're cute?"

"I'm irresistible, even now. Besides," he said, nodding towards the apartments on the hillside where the gunfire originated, "I was hoping your plan would get us out of this mess sooner rather than later."

Wood splinters erupted on either side of the boat, the air thick with the smell of salt and gunpowder. The shooter had pinned them, trying to bait them into the open. Gabriella's body tensed as they flattened themselves into the sand, their faces inches from the shoreline. The saltwater stung her lips, and Stone's voice, gravelly but calm, reached her ears.

"We need to split up," he said, his eyes darting across the hills, still scanning for the sniper. "I'll draw his fire. You get out— head to the deeper water."

Gabriella started to protest, but Stone cut her off with a raised hand.

"You're injured. You'll need more time to swim. Stay low, dive under the waves, and zigzag. Don't surface in a straight line, got it?"

She nodded, biting her lip. "Just don't get yourself killed, okay?"

Without waiting for the count, Gabriella darted into the water, her body slicing through the first wave. Bullets zipped past Stone's head, tracer rounds lighting the darkness like angry fireflies. He stood, boldly flipping the sniper the bird, before throwing himself into the surf. No way I'm dying like this, he thought as he hit the sea floor hard, the impact knocking the wind out of him.

In the distance, high above, Jambil cursed under his breath. He had been sloppy letting them get too far. Peering through his Russian-made rifle's scope, he saw their silhouettes slipping into the water. He had them now. Adjusting the sight, he muttered to himself, "Come up for air."

Jambil squeezed the trigger, his bullet tearing through the night. Wood splinters flew as the round hit near Stone's head. The sniper sneered. The wind was still—a perfect night to kill. Amateurs, he thought. His training in Egypt had taught him better, but the alcohol clouded his judgment, and tonight, he was careless.

Below, Stone fought against the ocean's pull, the courier bags wrapped around his body like shackles. He struggled, muscles straining, trying to free himself. The straps, soaked and tightened, had become a trap. A bullet struck the bag, the impact forcing him to dive under the surface again.

"Dammit!" Jambil spat, stamping his foot in frustration as he watched the target slip away again.

Stone surfaced, gasping for air. His lungs burned, his vision blurred from the saltwater, but he couldn't afford to stop. The knife in his pocket was his only chance. With swift, desperate motions, he sawed through the straps, but just as he was about to cut the last one, a hand tugged at the bag. He spun, ready to fight, and there was Gabriella beside him, her eyes fierce and determined. She jerked the bag free, and together they dove under again, their bodies moving as one.

The surface beckoned once again, but Gabriella broke through, her eyes catching sight of a dinghy cutting through the waves, fast and relentless. Were they friend or foe? Stone wondered. No time to think. He grabbed her, pulling them both under again as bullets sprayed the water. But Gabriella fought back, breaking away, and surfaced near the boat.

Stone followed, his knife ready, only to be greeted by the sight of men straddling the dinghy, their weapons aimed at the beach. The sniper had found them again, his shots pinging off the boat's side, but these men remain unflinching, their fire focused on the apartments on the hilltop. Gabriella was pulled aboard, and a man gestured for Stone to grab the rope. With a surge of adrenaline, Stone held on as the dinghy sped away, the force almost ripped his arm from its socket.

Time blurred. Stone felt his body being hauled aboard, his muscles aching, every breath labored. He collapsed next to Gabriella, her eyes closed but her pulse strong. "Don't worry, Doctor," she whispered, her voice hoarse but defiant. "I'll live."

Stone looked over at her as the sky behind them erupted. A rocket slammed into the hillside, and the apartment next to the building Jambil had been perched in crumbled inward, a fireball lighting up the night. The sniper's anger had cost him his position—and possibly his life.

Jambil staggered to his feet on the balcony, dazed, blood trickling from a gash on his forehead. His scope lay shattered beside him, the rifle useless. He had been reckless, foolish. He watched as the dinghy disappeared into the horizon, the firelight flickering in his haunted eyes.

He had failed. For the first time in years, he had lost his edge, and it terrified him.

As the dinghy bounced across the waves, Gabriella's hand found its way into Stone's, her grip weak but resolute. No matter what followed, they survived this night. But under the cover of night, the war raged on.

CHAPTER 43

INS Romach

The waves slapped the hull of the INS Romach, their rhythmic thud just audible over the steady hum of the engines as the missile ship cut through the ink-black Mediterranean night. Gabriella felt a pair of strong hands hoist her onto the deck, Stone directly behind. There was no celebration among the SEAL team that had rescued them. No high fives, no congratulations. The adrenaline still coursing through them, they understood that in every perfectly executed plan, the smallest unseen variable could upend everything. For now, surviving was victory enough.

In the ship's cramped medical bay below decks, a sense of sanctuary settled. The smell of antiseptic was acute in the air as medics worked fast, cleaning their cuts and bruises. Stone winced as a swab traced a deep scrape along his arm. As the ship steamed into the safety of the Mediterranean, turning south toward Haifa, the sense of lingering danger began to lift, though neither Stone nor Gabriella fully relaxed.

Port of Haifa, Pre-Dawn

The INS Romach glided into Haifa before sunrise, the docks eerily quiet in the early morning gloom. Its special cargo—Gabriella, Stone, and the SEAL team—was offloaded and the crew hurried away for debriefing. Every man aboard had been sworn to secrecy, under threat of being assigned the worst possible duty: walking ancient goat herders' routes in the Sinai. Israel's survival, its precarious existence surrounded by enemies, depended on such discretion.

Stone and Gabrella were cleared by Medical, both given a round of injectable antibiotics, TB and tenuous. Stone thought this was an overkill on being precautionary and told the acting Katzin akademai bakhi- medical officer his thoughts and was met with a stare of indifference. Stone tried again curse and berating the officer further telling him to give himself a round of shots in case he got dementia from STD while going on leave. Gabriella translated the final insult to the medical officer which caused him to break a slight smile before leaving.

Rubbing his backside, Stone stated "this becoming a pain in the."

"Yeah, yeah come on Tarzan let's get off the ship and get something to eat."

What? Tarzan? Where did that come from?"

"Oh, you didn't hear the crew named you that after the seal team described your feat of strength by holding onto the side of the dingy. They said it must have been true love you held on for so long." Gabriella smiled and winked pulling towards the exit.

"Great, whatever happened to the whole secrecy deal we were hammered with earlier?"

"Hey, you know how legends get started," laughing as they climbed the ladder to the top deck.

As they disembarked, Stone felt a strange unease. Israel was among the safest nations in the world, yet they just walk away—

no ID checks, no questions, no paperwork. A nagging thought tugged at the back of his mind, but it was interrupted by Gabriella's gleeful shout.

"Come on, slowpoke! I want you to meet someone!"

She was waving excitedly at a woman waiting near a sleek BMW SUV parked at the edge of the dock. The woman was tall, statuesque, with auburn hair that danced in the breeze. There was an air of grace and power about her, and Stone's primary thought was that she might have stepped out of a painting.

Gabriella embraced her with the force of a bear hug, both women laughing like schoolgirls. Stone, watching the display, felt like a man out of place—an observer in a world he could scarcely comprehend.

"Alright, perv," Gabriella teased, catching his gaze. "This is my best friend, Shoshana. Stop gawking and say hello."

Visibly flustered, Stone extended a hand, only to be pulled into a tight embrace. In rapid Hebrew, Shoshana thanked him for saving her friend and wished him many future children with Gabriella. Her blue eyes sparkled as she switched to English. "Gabriella has told me all about you. So, what does Tarzan like to eat?"

The nickname caught him off guard, and Gabriella couldn't contain her laughter. "Oh, you didn't know? The crew started calling you that after the SEAL team told them about your little feat of strength—holding onto the dinghy for dear life. They said it was love that kept you hanging on." She grinned, pulling him towards the car.

"Great, so much for secrecy."

"Legends have a way of spreading," she laughed, leading him up the gangplank.

As they drove away, the bustling port of Haifa receded into the background, and the tension of the previous twenty-four hours began to ebb. Shoshana weaved through the city with ease, her demeanor as relaxed as if they'd just come from a stroll on the beach, not a life-or-death mission. Stone couldn't help but marvel at the contrast. He had never seen people so adept at compartmentalizing trauma, so quick to embrace the joys of life in the face of ever-present threats.

The Mediterranean sun had already begun to warm the city by the time Shoshana turned onto a narrow street in the old port district. They pulled up outside Hanamal 12, an upscale restaurant housed in a former warehouse. The neighborhood, with its faded industrial grit, seemed at odds with the gourmet reputation of the place.

As they climbed the stairs, Stone couldn't shake the feeling that this was a world far removed from the chaos they had just survived. The restaurant's intimate setting, with Moroccan rugs on the walls and a view of the sea, was a stark contrast to the danger they had been in hours earlier. The scent of fresh seafood and spices filled the air as they walked to a table on the terrace overlooking the harbor.

Shoshana smiled, her hand lingering on Stone's arm. "You must try the shrimp with hummus and lime. Or the mushrooms stuffed with goat cheese. Everything here is special."

Stone nodded absently, still half-lost in his thoughts, as the server appeared to take their order. He watched Gabriella and

Shoshana laugh and tease each other, their easy camaraderie, a reminder of the deep bond they shared. Stone, in contrast, felt like a man on the outside looking in, still processing the events of the past hours.

As the meal arrived—plates piled with Mediterranean fish, grilled to perfection—Shoshana slipped into her role as tour guide, sharing stories about the restaurant's history. Stone listened, yet his attention was elsewhere, replaying the night's events, the gunfire, the mission, the precariousness of their survival.

Their laughter was interrupted by the arrival of Shlomi, the restaurant's owner, a short, stocky man with a contagious smile. More hugs, more rapid-fire Hebrew, and suddenly Stone found himself swept into the warm embrace of Israeli hospitality. It was jarring, this sudden shift from danger to levity, but maybe that was the point. In a land where conflict was ever-present, life had to be celebrated in the spaces between.

After the meal, Shoshana whisked them away, the SUV speeding through the streets like a bullet. Stone, wedged between the laughter of two women who had known each other for decades, felt the surrealness of the moment. Not twelve hours ago, they had been pinned down by enemy fire, and now, they were heading toward a beach house under the hot Israeli sun.

When they arrived, the house seemed ordinary enough, a whitewashed bungalow near the sea. But as Stone stepped inside, he noticed the subtle details: the reinforced walls, the anti-surveillance devices hidden in plain sight. Gabriella was already bustling around, opening windows, letting the sea breeze fill the space.

"So, what do you think?" she asked, her voice light but her eyes searching his face for something deeper.

Stone, ever the soldier, took it all in—the walls, the defenses, the hidden layers beneath the surface. But it was Gabriella, standing there with her fingers on her hips, a mischievous smile playing on her lips, who held his attention.

"I think," he said slowly, "that I've had about enough surprises for one day."

Gabriella grinned, her eyes glinting with something unreadable. "Oh, Stone. The surprises are just getting started."

And with that, the world outside—the mission, the danger, the unanswered questions—faded into the background, just for a short time.

CHAPTER 44

The Test

Days and nights blended into an unbroken haze for Stone. He found solace in the rhythm of waking up with Gabriella, their intense physical connection blurring the hours. Sex, nourishment, and then more sex—became a pattern of distraction that kept them from the darker thoughts lurking in the corners of their minds. Afterward, in the quiet moments, Gabriella would open up, telling Stone about her ties to Mossad and how she'd been strategically placed at the camp. Conversations often drifted to the children they both missed. Each time, Stone's face would harden, the shadows deepening around his eyes, and he'd shift the subject, usually with fresh sex—an escape from the sadness he couldn't shake. Gabriella sensed it all too well. She understood his pain, how he wasn't ready to move on, and she knew what had to be done, regardless of her affection for him.

Three weeks passed. Gabriella resumed her morning runs, though she returned each time limping, her face betraying a grimace. Stone would massage her muscles, his fingers digging deep until the spasms eased. Gabriella would cook exquisite fish dishes, their evenings concluding with passionate intimacy. It was a fragile peace, a period of rest and recovery that couldn't last.

One morning, Gabriella pushed herself harder on her run, determined to beat the pain. The bungalow came into view, but today something was off. Two silver Land Rovers, with their engines still running, parked at odd angles—one on each side of the street, positioned for surveillance. The dark-tinted windows offered no clues, but Gabriella's instincts screamed danger. She could try to make it to the gate or blow past them and sprint toward the crowded beach. Her heart raced.

Unbeknownst to her, Stone had been watching. He always timed his martial arts workout to finish just as she returned. Today, though, he had noticed the SUVs arrived ten minutes earlier. No one exited. It was the third day in a row, and each time, they left before Gabriella appeared. Stone's operational experience allowed him to identify a surveillance team. Something wasn't right—no foot soldiers, no one walking the perimeter. That was sloppy. And dangerous.

He'd searched the house for weapons during Gabriella's runs, turning up nothing. One night, he sense a faint vibration while stretching his legs against the wall. No air conditioning was on, and the windows were always ajar at night—a vulnerability that unsettled him. He suspected the house was bugged but found no cameras or mics when Gabriella playfully teased him about his cleaning.

As Gabriella neared the closest SUV, the front doors opened simultaneously. Two large men stepped out—brutish, military types, with cropped hair and ill-fitting shirts that strained against their bulging muscles. The driver raised a hand, signaling her to stop. Gabriella, now only two meters away, paused, her breath coming in short gasps. She just had time to notice the blur of motion behind the driver.

In a flash, Stone's hand shot out, locking around the driver's collar and yanking him backward into a brutal guillotine choke. The man's eyes widened in shock as his feet left the ground. He had no time to reach for his weapon before Stone flung him like a ragdoll onto the hood of the SUV, denting the metal with a sickening thud.

Stone was on the second man before he could react. The thug fumbled for his gun, but Stone's vice-like grip immobilized his hand. Stone twisted the man's wrist, forcing him to bend at the waist, and swept his legs out from under him with a modified judo throw. The man hit the ground with bone-rattling force, groaning in agony as Stone retrieved his gun.

"Bravo, bravo," a voice rang out, heavy with amusement. Across the street stood a stocky older man, his graying hair clipped short. Flanking him stood four leaner men, two of whom had Uzis trained on Stone. The others scanned the area for threats.

The elderly man strolled forward, his smile wide and unsettling. Gabriella waved Stone down, signaling him to lower the weapon as she approached the mature man with contained anger.

"Hello, Mammala. How are you?" the man asked, his tone dripping with familiarity. Before Gabriella responded, the man pulled her into an embrace, planting kisses on her cheeks with exaggerated affection.

General Moscha Bondmann. Stone's body tensed as Gabriella allowed the general to drape his arm around her. Bondmann turned to Stone, eyes gleaming with recognition.

"So, this is the great Tarzan," the general drawled in accented English, his tone mocking but tinged with respect.

"Introduce me, deary, to the man you've been holed up with."

Gabriella retreated back, embarrassed, but her words in Hebrew sharp and quick. Stone caught fragments but understood the message: they were lucky it was Stone who intervened, not her. If it had been her, they would all be dead.

The general laughed heartily, his booming voice filling the street. He shook Stone's hand with surprising vigor. "She's right, of course. You handled yourself well. Sorry for the rough introduction, but I had to see you for myself."

The men retrieved their injured comrades, grumbling as they loaded them into the SUVs. The general gave orders in rapid Hebrew before turning back to Stone and Gabriella. "Breakfast tomorrow, Gabriella. That little café on the beach. Ten a.m. sharp." He winked before retreating into his vehicle. The convoy pulled away, leaving the street eerily quiet once more.

Gabriella let out a sigh, her face tense with frustration. Stone stepped closer. "Want to explain what that was?"

"Not now," she muttered. "I need a shower... and something for my headache."

Stone watched her closely. "I have a remedy for both."

Gabriella shot him a tired smile. "Where do you get the energy? You didn't even break a sweat."

He grinned. "Worked in a restaurant once. Had to carry sacks of flour."

They both laughed, the tension easing a little. But as they entered the house, Stone's mind raced. Something wasn't adding up, and he needed answers.

Later, after a quiet dinner, Gabriella broke the silence. "It wasn't your fault. I tried to keep them away. I thought—" Her voice cracked, eyes shimmering with unshed tears.

"It was a test, wasn't it?" Stone demanded. "Why?"

Gabriella hesitated, glancing at the walls. "Let's go for a walk," she spoke softly, gesturing for him to follow her outside.

The Mediterranean breeze was a welcome relief, but it did nothing to cool the tension between Stone and Gabriella. The rhythmic crash of the waves against the shore only heightened the uneasy silence as they walked along the sand, their bodies close but not in affection. A performance—two people pretending to be lovers, holding each other tightly, not out of care, but necessity. Stone's trained eye picked up their watchers: a man with a dog, awkwardly pulling the leash in a way no real pet owner would, and two more lurking in the shadows behind a vendor stand.

"This is my life," Gabriella muttered, her voice edged with frustration. "Always people watching over me."

"Watching out for you, or watching you?" Stone shot back; his tone laced with cynicism. "What are you? Some politician's rebellious daughter, running off to dangerous places just to piss off the family?"

The words stung. Gabriella whipped away from him, cursing in multiple languages, a furious symphony that told Stone he'd hit the mark. Without a word, she broke into a run down the shoreline, sand kicking up in her wake. Stone didn't chase her— he didn't need to. He knew exactly where she would end up.

When he returned to the bungalow, his belongings— carefully folded—were already packed in a small backpack by the gate. The house itself was dark, the shutters closed tight like a fortress. The message was clear. Without a second glance at the bag, Stone walked off, whistling sharply as he disappeared into the narrow streets. He knew the watchers would report his every move, but he didn't care. He was already thinking two steps ahead.

Gabriella tossed and turned through the night, the absence of Stone's presence gnawing at her. She hated to admit it, but she'd grown used to him being there. By morning, the frustration lingered, thick in the air. She dressed quickly, pulled her hair into a messy knot, and set out for a run, hoping the physical exertion would help clear her mind. But it didn't. Not while she anticipated facing the General.

CHAPTER 45

Revelation

Cutting across the crowded marketplace, Gabriella arrived at the beachfront restaurant where the General had insisted on meeting. She spotted the usual watchers stationed around—eyes always on her, always waiting. The sound of laughter hit her as she walked inside the shaded patio. The General, mid-story, stopped as soon as he saw her.

"You're late," he said flatly, his jovial demeanor disappearing behind a stony gaze.

Gabriella wiped the sweat from her brow with a cloth napkin, her chest heaving from the exertion. "Traffic was bad," she replied sarcastically, dropping into a seat.

The General's laugh was loud, forced, and dismissive. He didn't want excuses. "Let's not dwell on it. I'm starving," waving the waiter over. "They make the best omelet here. Even that white-only nonsense you call an omelet." His eyes narrowed as he spoke, trying to maintain the guise of a casual breakfast.

They ate in relative silence, though the General spoke endlessly, as if just breakfast between old comrades. It wasn't until they finished that he brought up what was in truth on his mind.

"That boy of yours… Stone, was it? Smart. A doctor, too. And Jewish. But not the one for you," he said with a shrug, taking a prolonged sip from his glass. "You're lucky you sent him packing."

Gabriella's voice dropped low, almost lost beneath the sound of the ocean breeze and the whirring fan overhead. "He could have been the one," she professed, her words trembling. "But you chased him away. And for that, I will never forgive you."

The General leaned in, his eyes hard as steel, waiting for the rest. But Gabriella wiped away a stray tear and exhaled, fighting the urge to break down.

With a crisp smile, the General slid a manila envelope across the table. "He's not so innocent, your Tarzan." He tapped the top of the file with a single finger, the weight of its contents weighty between them. "CIA, Special Forces, a mercenary in everything but name. He's no saint, but not beyond redemption, either."

Gabriella hesitated before grabbing the envelope, her fingers trembling. The General's tone softened, though his words remained firm. "You'll see for yourself. He's too independent, too much of a wild card for our tastes. Read it. You'll understand."

He stood, his large frame casting a shadow over her. "When you're done, you know what to do with the file," he added, his voice cold, final. He placed a kiss on each of her cheeks and left without another word, his bodyguards close behind, scanning the perimeter as if expecting an ambush at any moment.

Back at the bungalow, Gabriella methodically packed her things, her mind racing with the contents of the file she hadn't yet opened. The clothes she'd bought for Stone sat on the bed, folded neatly. She couldn't bring herself to throw them away. Not yet.

A sleek, black Mercedes sat idling at the curb, its driver

already gripping the gun on his lap, eyes scanning the street for any sign of danger. Word had spread about the confrontation the day before, and the driver was determined not to make the same mistakes his colleagues had. Gabriella caught his eye in the rearview mirror, and he hurriedly popped the trunk without stepping out. No one was taking any risks today.

Gabriella, dressed in a simple yellow sundress, loaded her bags into the trunk herself and slid into the backseat. She pulled her sunglasses down over her eyes and leaned back, crossing her legs, the Mediterranean breeze flowing through the cracked windows.

It was going to be a extensive, silent ride to Tel Aviv.

The General's words echoed in her mind. Stone was further than he seemed—more than she had known. As the Mercedes cruised down the boulevard, she rested her hand on the manila envelope, wondering how much of Stone's past was buried inside. The truth, she knew, was only a page away, but some truths were more dangerous than lies.

CHAPTER 46

Paris Friday Morning Current Day

The Louvre stirred with early morning activity, the hum of preparations echoing through its vast halls before the first visitor would arrive at the iconic glass pyramid entrance. But the East Wing, the museum's quieter side, held an entrance known to true aficionados. Hidden in plain sight, it offered a swift, uninterrupted path into the labyrinthine exhibits. Today, however, a sense of unease lingered in the air, greater than usual routine tension of maintenance and repairs.

A tarp hung loosely over the freshly sealed crack in the wall, the result of overnight repairs. It would take three days, maybe greater, before the final touches could be made. The night officer on duty made his usual report, noting the extended drying time before sending off an email to the wing's curator. Yet, two of his staff had not reported in this morning. One absence, that of a janitor, was swiftly dismissed. But Monsieur Chartrand's absence—peculiar. He'd worked here for years, never late, never absent, and had scarcely taken a vacation in the past five years.

"Should someone check on him?" Ms. Cropton suggested, her concern evident, though quickly brushed aside by the head of personnel with a dismissive wave. "Maybe he got lucky," he laughed, before ending the conversation. She shook her head and turned her attention to the shortage of Chinese-speaking interpreters for today's tours. Her thoughts shifted as she dialed a freelance agency, wondering how they'd manage yet again with ill-prepared guides.

But behind the polished facade, something darker was brewing. Unseen, unheard, waiting to be unleashed.

CHAPTER 47

The Reunion

The Lufthansa flight from Tel Aviv landed at Charles de Gaulle Airport ahead of schedule. Gabriella passed through security, her embassy papers ensuring a smooth passage. She spent ten minutes weaving through the duty-free shops, blending with the crowd, executing counter-surveillance as she scanned for any tails. Satisfied, she made her way to the exit, eyes darting across the bustling terminal.

A sleek black van slid to a halt at the curb as she emerged. The door opened, revealing the grin of a blonde Australian operative. "Sorry, Sheila, back seat for you," he quipped, his smile broad and unashamedly irritating. Gabriella ignored the taunt, pushing her sunglasses down over her eyes as she stepped inside, the door slamming shut behind her.

The van sped off, the driver navigating Parisian traffic with a reckless precision that reminded her of home. Inside, three men, muscular and silent, occupied the seats, their eyes keen, assessing the situation as they neared their rendezvous. Each had their task, and they had rehearsed the plan until it was second nature.

One by one, the team disembarked, disappearing into the city, cautious of the surveillance web that blanketed Paris. Their final destination: a safe house on Rue Saint-André des Arts, tucked discreetly above Corcoran's Irish pub on the west bank.

The location was strategic, a stone's throw from the Île de la Cité and the Louvre.

Once inside, they debriefed, weapons and communication gear laid out with the meticulous care of seasoned operatives. Israel's intelligence had set this operation in motion, and now it was up to them to make sure nothing went wrong.

Gabriella walked after the meeting to the hotel with her overnight bag. Meeting with the Egyptian ambassador and said buyer started at 4pm. The plan was to convince them Israel was willing to buy back paintings they all knew came from its citizens and families for generations. No need for bidders, they were ready to pay top dollar for the stolen loot to save time for all parties. Such a meeting would be unthinkable going through official government channels. The ambassador stood to gain a large bonus for brokering such a meeting between the parties. When he brought the news to the sellers, he was at once accused of being an Israel spy, a traitor. Sabre wanted to kill him on the spot. But calmer heads prevailed, and the older man agreed to the primary talks. He was told to ask for even more money for the exchange.

Gabriella's mission was delicate. The ambassador she was meeting was no stranger to backdoor dealings. He had brokered the sale of priceless stolen artifacts—a deal so secret that even government channels were kept in the dark. Israel had intervened at the final minute, offering an obscene amount to buy back the treasures and avoid an international scandal. But the ambassador's greed had complicated matters. He wanted more, far more than what was on the table.

Now, negotiations would begin. The stakes remain high, not just for Gabriella, but for Israel. Failure was not an option.

CHAPTER 48

The Raid

While Gabriella's team moved in silence, elsewhere in Paris, a second operation was underway.

The Israelis had intercepted key intelligence after capturing David, a CIA asset compromised by Stone. An Israeli team had been tailing the Americans from the time they picked David up at the airport and the arrival of Stone at the building used for interrogations. The Team saw Stone leave the building alone. They understood the layout of the building from joint task forces with the Americans on different occasions.

The young guard who overwhelmed from the morning events didn't try to stop them. Israels' flashed their ID's and had no trouble extracting David from one remaining AMerican who opened the secured doors. He was nursing it appeared to be a facial injury with an ice pack and a beer in his opposite hand.

Under duress, he revealed vital information—locations of Arab terrorist cells, warehouses packed with munitions, artifacts, and the timing of attacks that could devastate Paris. David, bruised and shaken, pleaded in Hebrew as they whisked him away. "Keep me in Israel. Don't send me back."

Israel's top brass, already stretched thin, knew they couldn't act alone. They reached out to the French anti-terrorism task force, securing a collaboration that would put boots on the ground within hours. The French president authorized full cooperation, giving the Israelis free rein to lead the mission. It wasn't just about averting an attack; it was about dismantling an entire network before it could strike.

David's intel pointed to a warehouse on the outskirts of the 11th arrondissement—a nondescript building that, to the casual observer, would seem abandoned. But hidden inside were the tools of destruction, waiting for the precise moment to be unleashed on the city.

As the teams converged on their target, the clock ticked down. There was no room for error, no margin for delay. Every step was calculated, every movement deliberate. They moved in unison, a well-oiled machine, poised to strike.

Raids occurred on the two warehouses and four apartment complexes on the outer borough of Paris. The discovery includes over 200 pieces of artwork and sculptures. The pre-dawn raids executed by French and Israel special task force divisions, capturing 12 people, five on the no-fly list for internal travel. Neighbors woke up to the sounds of doors being smashed open as the sunrise peaked from the edges of the rooftops. Several streets were blocked off in anticipation of the early dawn raids with police roping off access. Nearby streets had patrols checking for residents' identifications before allowed through to their homes. A taxi parked out of the perimeter, car still running sat Yoisse watching the raids unfold. Fidgeting with the door locks and quick glances at his watch made the driver nervous of his passenger. They had cost Yoisse millions of Euros and assets, men he had trained for years for an event like this tonight. Greed had taken over his employer and cost them millions and possibly their freedom.

He left the driver a large tip for waiting and excited the vehicle and darted across the street to the metro entrance.

Rue Saint-André des Arts

Gabriella entered the Egyptian ambassador's office, her heartbeat steady despite the tension in the room. He was flanked by two men, hulking shadows that loomed with menace. On the table in front of him, a manila envelope lay open with the terms for the return of the artifacts in questions with photos of each as well as a picture of Stone. She was aware of its contents and the outrageous dollar amount to be paid in Euros. What she didn't expect was the picture of Stone and one paragraph only underneath.

"You're late," the ambassador remarked, his voice cold. Gabriella offered no apology, sitting across from him, her eyes scanning the room for any sign of deception. This meeting was a high-stakes game, one wrong move, and it could all collapse.

"I don't have time for your theatrics," her voice low and controlled. "Let's get to business."

The ambassador leaned back, a smile playing at the corner of his lips. "You Israelis... always so eager to close the deal." He slid the dossier toward her, his eyes gleaming with satisfaction. "But this one... this one's special."

Gabriella reviewed the file, her stomach tightening as she read the details. No outward emotions displayed on her face. Stone's history was laid bare, from his days as a Special Forces operative to his clandestine work with the CIA. The general had been right—he wasn't innocent. But it was never about innocence. It was about leverage. The Israeli government as a last resort would pay if the warehouse search turned up empty. What did Stone have to do with any of this? Her thoughts interrupted.

"Adding this man to the payment will safely secure the artifacts you need. I also capped the price to go no higher, you are welcome" the ambassador said, with full of convince.

"What makes you think we can delivery this man to you?"

"You are not the sole government with assets and resources around the world." He muttered dismissive of the question.

Gabriella didn't reply. She didn't need to. She needed to contact the branch office on this latest development and keep things in motion without missing any deadlines. Standing from her chair, and a slight bow of her head she spun around and headed out the door and out onto the street, knowing she had tails to shake off before meeting with the team and the upcoming meeting scheduled.

CHAPTER 49

Paris, Friday Evening

Yoise entered the narrow alley that led to the flat, a rented place provided by a well-connected network of Lebanese expats. Every step was deliberate. He scanned the streets and windows above, noting every shadow and light shift, his pulse steady, his instincts sharp. Over half an hour of backtracking, darting across boulevards, and weaving through side streets reassured him—he wasn't followed. Satisfied, he slipped into the brownstone on the boulevard. The 8th arrondissement wasn't exactly discreet, but his employers had a taste for the unusual—this row of brownstones stood out amidst Paris' classical architecture. A beacon for trouble, in Yoise's opinion. But he wasn't paid to offer opinions.

Inside, the cool air hit him as he locked the door, his senses relaxing. He had three hours, maybe less, before the meeting at the Ritz. Time enough to catch some sleep and shower away the day's sweat.

The Ritz Hotel—famous, decadent, the haunt of the elite. On 15 Place Vendôme, security around the Ritz was tighter than any embassy. The moment Yoise entered the lobby, the smell of polished marble and expensive cologne assaulted him. Every inch of the place screamed wealth and secrecy. Management had invested heavily in security—discreetly hidden bomb barriers, bulletproof windows masquerading as elegant glass. The kind of precautions only the wealthiest could afford.

As Yoise made his way toward the Salon Proust, he allowed himself to blend into the atmosphere. The air was thick with money, whispers of power exchanges, and the palpable sense that behind every smile was a knife waiting to be drawn. He wasn't here to indulge, though. His employers—wealthy, powerful, and dangerously paranoid—waited.

Shakibe Arslan, Lebanese royalty in title if not in reality, had clawed his way to the top. His family, a relic of a fallen era, fled Lebanon generations ago. Now, they operated like shadow kings across Europe and Asia, amassing wealth through every means imaginable: oil, shipping, arms, even art. This meeting, conversely, dealt with a far more ominous subject.

Yoise reached the Salon Proust and paused. The room, with its plush armchairs and faint lighting, felt more like a British drawing room. A deceptive comfort. He was relieved not to see the dreaded senior man or Samurai—the cousin notorious for his love of decapitation. Instead, Drewee Fakhry awaited him, third in line to the imaginary throne, as spoiled and unpredictable as ever.

The fireplace crackled, it wasn't cold enough to justify a fire, however. Drewee insisted on it anyway. Typical.

"Ah, Yoise! How's my half-brother today?" Drewee grinned, a smile that never reached his eyes. The men seated around him—all multi-millionaires and loyal only to Drewee— chuckled at the false warmth in the greeting. Yoise gave a stiff nod, sizing them up.

No chair was offered to him. The dynamic was clear: Yoise was the outsider. These men saw him as a tool, a necessary evil in their play for power. Drewee, lounging with the arrogance of a man who had never been denied anything, leaned forward, his smirk widening.

"Well, what do you have for us?"

Yoise's eyes flicked to the table, then back to Drewee. Silently, he pulled two keycards from his pocket and tossed them on the polished wood. The room went quiet. The massive man to Drewee's right picked one up, inspecting it carefully, then glancing at Yoise before handing it to Drewee. The tension in the room thickened as the silence dragged on.

Drewee tilted his head, mockingly. "What's this? Speak, Yoise, or shall we assume a camel has more to say than you?" He laughed, the sound cruel, and the group followed suit, their laughter hollow and uncomfortable.

Yoise remained impassive. He'd seen worse men than Drewee fall, and he wasn't here to entertain their childish games.

The keycards held the access to a secure storage facility on the outskirts of Paris—a facility housing something far more valuable than money. Inside pieces of art stolen from museums across Europe, artifacts worth millions on the black market. The cards were the prize, the culmination of months of surveillance, bribes, and killings.

"The keys to your future fortune," Yoise spoke, his voice low, his words sharp. The laughter stopped. Drewee's eyes narrowed, the weight of Yoise's statement sinking in.

"Where?" Drewee asked, the mocking tone gone, replaced

by the greed that fueled him.

"An industrial warehouse in the 11th arrondissement," Yoise said. "You'll find what you're looking for there. But be careful—security is tight. Cameras everywhere. And others are watching."

Drewee's grin returned, this time colder, more calculating. "Others?"

"The Israelis," Yoise replied, his gaze hard. "They've monitored the sale's progress for several weeks. They know something big is going down, and they'll stop at nothing to get their hands on those artifacts."

The room shifted with unease. Drewee's smile faltered for a moment before returning. "Then we'll just have to make sure they don't live long enough to enjoy the view."

Yoise's muscles tightened, but he kept his face blank. Drewee's arrogance would get them all killed if he wasn't careful. But that wasn't Yoise's problem. He'd done his job. Now, it was up to these men to figure out how to survive the storm heading their way.

As he left the Salon Proust, Yoise glanced back once, catching Drewee's eyes. The two men locked gazes, and in that moment, Yoise knew—when the time came, one of them wouldn't walk away.

CHAPTER 50

Spa Treatment

Catherine tried on the last of the dresses, twirling in front of the mirror. Stone, glancing at his watch, already had the next part of the day lined up. He picked up the phone, dialing the spa. "An appointment for Cathrine, two hours from now," he said. Catherine raised a brow.

"You know that wasn't serious, right?" dalf-smiling, recalling her joke from the lobby.

Stone's face remained unreadable. "Enjoy yourself. There's a hairdresser available afterward. I've some calls to make, plus I need to find a tux. That'll take me a couple of hours."

She hesitated before agreeing. After trying on two additional dresses and modeling them once again for Stone, she left with her room key, confirming they'd meet at 7 p.m. in the lobby. Stone nodded. He watched her walk out the door knowing all to well the time crunch.

Stone showered quick, throwing on brown trousers and a high-end navy pullover. His brown boat shoes matched the casual, well-heeled Parisian look he aimed for. He grabbed a handful of hundred Euros, a burner phone from his bag, and a leather jacket. As he left the room, he avoided the elevator, opting for the rear stairwell. His gut told him to be cautious. He had already spotted two individuals in the lobby earlier, flanked by heavy security. It was too much of a coincidence for Gabriella to be there, not to mention Sebastian—a ghost from the past. Stone hadn't seen him in over three years, yet there was no mistaking the figure, even with burn scars that marred his face.

The last time Stone saw Sebastian was after the explosion at the refugee compound. The blast had been devastating, leaving a crater where the building once stood. Following the gunfire, he and Gabriella had a narrow escape. They hadn't stayed to check for survivors. But here was Sebastian, alive and apparently working with the Lebanese security team.

Stone couldn't shake the questions swirling in his mind. Why was Gabriella talking to him? It couldn't be random—not in a place like this, not with the auction happening tonight. Stone needed answers, and the individual who could help him untangle this mess was WeisBerger.

Exiting through the hotel's kitchen corridor, Stone bypassed the main doors and slipped out through the loading dock. A pair of security guards stationed at the exit hardly looked his way. Dressed as he was, Stone blended in with the hotel's upscale clientele, striding with confidence. His father's old lesson echoed in his mind: Act like you belong, and no one will ask questions. And if they do, bullshit your way through.

Out in the open air, S A late afternoon chill settled over Paris, and Stone felt it. He cut across Rue de Rivoli, angling toward Tour Saint-Jacques park. The park buzzed with activity—schoolchildren playing, mothers chatting, dog walkers ambling about. The scene had a rhythm to it, but Stone's trained eyes scanned for anything out of place. He circled the park, sitting briefly on different benches, checking for any signs of surveillance. Nothing. The pattern of motion was natural, and no one seemed interested in him.

Satisfied, he pulled out his burner phone and dialed from memory. WeisBerger's line rang once before a gruff voice answered.

"No truffles left," Stone said, keeping his tone casual.

"You're joking, right? I was counting on those," WeisBerger grumbled. Stone smirked, knowing full well they were being monitored by French authorities. The Prefecture de Police, with its satellite dishes and eavesdropping technology, likely had an operator listening in on every word.

"Well, I'm still waiting in the park. No delivery in sight," Stone replied, his eyes flicking toward the looming police building across the river. WeisBerger's team had a GPS beacon on his burner phone, tracking him within meters. They were aware of both his whereabouts and his challenges.

"So, it's that kind of party?" WeisBerger's voice shifted, more serious now. "Email me the details later. For now, what's the situation?"

"The merchandise is secure, but it's not making it to the auction tonight. Too many heavy hitters have shown up. I'm in over my head here. I need passes for tonight's event and maybe a little backup." Stone paused, waiting for a response.

There was silence on the other end, extensive enough to make Stone uneasy. Then WeisBerger's voice came through, low and ominous. "You need to move. You got company headed your way."

"Am I on my own?"

"Hard to say, don't lose your phone."

Stone stood from the bench, casually strolling toward the Seine. "Oh, one more thing," keeping his voice light, "I ran into an old girlfriend... and a ghost."

WeisBerger's response was almost amused. "A ghost, huh? Hope you can swim."

The line went dead.

Stone's eyes darted to the Pont d'Arcole bridge ahead of him. Tourists clogged the walkway, snapping selfies and crowding the narrow passage. The river below churned with boat traffic, chilly and uninviting. Behind him, uniformed police began setting up barriers at both ends of the bridge on Qual aux Fleus. Locals just glanced at the disruption, accustomed to such security measures in the city. But Stone knew this wasn't routine. This was a trap closing in around him.

His gut clenched as two black SUVs with tinted windows screeched to a halt on the far side of the bridge. Tactical teams spilled out, rifles drawn, moving with military precision. Stone didn't wait. He darted to the edge of the bridge, shoving aside a group of tourists as he vaulted over the railing.

He didn't make it far.

The stun gun hit him mid-air, sending electric currents searing through his body. Pain exploded in his nerves as new tasers hit him, one after another. His muscles seized, locking him in place as he hit the ground hard.

Hands grabbed on him before he could even process the

fall. Rough, unrelenting hands slapped plastic cuffs on his wrists and ankles, hog-tying him. Stone hardly registered the pain before he was lifted, carried like a sack of grain into a nearby waiting SUV. The entire takedown took less than a minute.

Tourists stood frozen, shocked by the speed and brutality of the operation. But as fast as it happened, life returned to normal. Cameras clicked, smiles returned, and the sightseers resumed their photos, unaware of the storm gathering around them.

As Stone lay in the back of the SUV, every muscle still burning from the tasers, He was certain of one thing, tonight's auction was going to be far more dangerous than he'd anticipated.

CHAPTER 51

The Arena

Stone woke up to the cutting sting of ice-cold water splashing over his face and back, the rancid stench of the sewer clinging to every breath. He jolted involuntarily, his battered body reacting in spasms to the frigid shock. His hands were cuffed behind him, his legs shackled, every joint screaming in pain from repeated blows. The bastards had beaten him unconscious and hadn't stopped there. He blinked through his swollen left eye, his right not much better but able to open, taking in the dull reflection of a shallow puddle on the cement floor beneath him. The air was thick with dampness, the cold gnawing at his bones. They had to be underground, probably in one of Paris' many forgotten tunnels.

His tormentors had tied his shirt around his head, periodically dousing him with water, each splash accompanied by further barrage of punches. He remembered the cycles—pain, suffocation, and darkness—broken only when they stepped away for a smoke break. The acrid scent of cheap Turkish cigarettes still lingered in the air, mingling with the foul reek of urine. Stone just hoped the latter wasn't his.

Shifting onto his right side, he spotted a bucket—likely the source of the smell—its contents splashed carelessly on the floor. Agony shot through his right shoulder as he moved, the arm dangling uselessly, probably dislocated. His head pounded from dehydration and the relentless abuse. He wasn't dead yet. That meant they wanted something.

Footsteps echoed down the corridor, the clatter of cheap shoes striking the cement, bringing with them a foul mix of sweat and bad cologne. Six pairs of legs appeared, and Stone's captors surrounded him again. One figure approached, the distinct click of expensive leather shoes giving him away. The man knelt beside him and slapped Stone hard across the face, drawing laughter from the rest. The blow came again, but Stone twisted his head just in time, letting the hand strike his skull instead. The man winced silently—perhaps not used to such resistance—but showed no further sign of pain.

The faint beam of a phone's flashlight illuminated Stone's bruised and swollen face. They took a picture, then the light blinked out. Stone caught bits of their conversation; rapid Arabic exchanges punctuated by laughter. A wheelchair was rolled in, and they hoisted him roughly into it, securing him with a chest strap. He was pushed forward, through the dim corridor, his body jolting with every bump.

As they ascended a series of ramps, the air shifted to some degree—cooler, fresher. They must be close to the surface. Stone's mind raced, tracking each turn, noting every faint detail of their route. The pushers, out of breath, mocked by their comrades, their banter lost on Stone, whose focus sharpened on his surroundings. They reached a chained gate, the metallic clank of keys signaling their passage through, and continued the grueling march.

They emerged at an elevator, its sleek, modern design incongruous with the subterranean filth they'd just left behind.

The corpulent odor of the sewer receded as they moved inside. Stone glanced at his reflection in the mirrored doors—his face a grotesque mask of bruises and cuts, his right arm hanging limp. He saw the man in the expensive shoes, Yoise, nod and wink in the reflection, a predator savoring his prey.

Yoise pressed his hand onto Stone's injured shoulder, sending a white-hot jolt of pain through him. Stone's vision blurred, but he kept his face impassive, refusing to give the man the satisfaction of hearing him scream.

"I'd prefer it was me," Yoise whispered in English, his voice soft but menacing. "I'd show you no mercy, and I'm sure you wouldn't either."

Stone didn't respond. The doors slid open to reveal a grand hall, its opulence a stark contrast to the hellish underworld he'd just been dragged through. Rows of chairs—hundreds of them—formed a semi-circle, half of them filled with an audience speaking in hushed tones. A massive, ornate rug covered the floor in the center, its rich colors and intricate patterns marred by dark stains Stone didn't need to guess the origin of. Four towering men in suits stood sentinel at the corners, their eyes locked on him.

On a raised platform to the left, five King Louis IV style golden thrones sat elevated above the scene, their Baroque grandeur fitting for royalty—or executioners. To the right, an electronic scoreboard ticked numbers up and down—bets, no doubt, placed on whatever horrific spectacle was about to unfold. The letters "A" and "B" flickered on the board, a grotesque parody of a sporting event.

As he was wheeled toward the center of the room, the

crowd's chatter grew louder, a low hum of excitement. Stone was lifted from the wheelchair and forced to stand, his legs shaking from exhaustion and pain. Classical music swelled from hidden speakers—Mozart's Don Giovanni Overture, of all things—and Stone knew with cold certainty that this was a death arena. The rug of chance, or perhaps the rug of justice. Either way, he was the main event.

The audience rose to their feet as a procession of dignitaries in colorful, ceremonial garb entered the hall. Stone's head was forced into a bow, his muscles screaming in protest as he held the humiliating position. His captors, brutish men, took pleasure in making him suffer. When the music ceased, an older man in the center raised his hand, commanding silence. A man, dressed in traditional Arab attire, stepped forward with a microphone and addressed the crowd in Arabic. Stone caught fragments of the speech, but the message was clear: he was one of the "interfering parties" from the museum heist. The scoreboard switched to video footage—five men with plastic bags over their heads, suffocating as they thrashed against their restraints. The crowd erupted in cheers as the gruesome film played out, the men's agonizing deaths broadcast for the sick pleasure of these elites.

When the video ended, the speaker gestured toward Stone, and the audience roared with approval. But before the madness could continue, a woman stepped forward, her voice cutting through the chaos. She spoke in French, her tone commanding attention.

"This man is injured," she stated plainly, her voice devoid of fear. "The odds should reflect that, wouldn't you say?"

The room fell silent, and a murmur of agreement rippled

through the crowd. The leader on the platform nodded, and the betting board flickered, the odds jumping from 50 to 1 to 80 to 1.

Stone clenched his fists, flexing his injured arm to restore circulation. He took a deep breath, centering himself as he kneeled on the rug, adopting the calm, ready posture of seiza. To the untrained eye, he looked defenseless, broken. But in reality, he was coiled, every muscle prepared for the inevitable clash. His body might be battered, but his mind was alert, prepared for anything that followed.

The guards surrounding him had no idea what was coming.

CHAPTER 52

The Champion

Stone's intuition proved correct. The behemoth standing before him wasn't just muscle; he was a former Olympian, a wrestler and powerlifter once celebrated by Lebanon. Fame had been brief, though, brought by injuries and a steroid scandal that cut his career short. With no future in sports and hardly any job prospects, especially for a 300-pound enforcer with more brawn than brains, the family had found him a role—security, theft, and, eventually, the bloody business of the underground fighting circuit. He became a legend for snapping necks, a new kind of notoriety that brought him wealth, women, and a twisted sense of pride. Tonight, he intended to add another notch to his record by breaking the neck of an American.

The man pounded his chest like a caged beast, riling the crowd. His face turned crimson with exertion and rage. Sweat dripped from his forehead as he bellowed a primal scream, preparing to charge.

Stone, still kneeling on the rug, kept his breathing steady, his one good eye tracking every movement. His body, though battered, was coiled like a spring.

For his size, the former Olympian was surprisingly fast, closing the four-meter gap in seconds. Stone could feel the raw power emanating from him—he was all brute force, set on smashing Stone to pieces. The man's intent was clear: lock him up, break his limbs, then strangle the life out of him. He thrived on the screams of his victims, and Stone was supposed to be no different.

But Stone wasn't most men.

As the giant lunged through the air, Stone sensed the shift in the air pressure. His senses heightened, the adrenaline sharpening his focus to a razor's edge. The crowd's collective gasp narrowly registered as Stone pivoted sharply to the left, moving a split second before the brute's body slammed into the spot where he'd been kneeling.

The impact reverberated through the room, the audience tense in anticipation of the carnage that didn't happen. Some gasped; few cursed. The woman who had earlier voiced concern gripped her chair, knuckles white as her gaze flicked between the combatants and the nearest exit, trapped between the spectacle and the horror.

The giant, caught off guard by Stone's unexpected agility, hit the hard tile floor with a thud. His left hand brushed Stone's leg, but it was too late. His massive form slammed into the ground; the shock visible in his eyes as he realized he hadn't crushed his target. Getting up pursuing his prey again in a half squat stance, Stone was already moving fluid as water, launching an upward strike—a perfectly aimed age zuki punch into the man's groin.

The wrestler's scream was guttural, primal, as his right testicle exploded in pain. He instinctively cupped himself, his body curling involuntarily as his forehead and right shoulder smashed into the floor. The crowd collectively winced as the giant writhed on the ground, his face contorted in agony. He struggled to stand again, but when he did, he faced the audience, still gripping his groin, unaware that Stone was already behind him.

Stone's breathing was steady now, his heart rate lowered as he moved in with surgical precision. The Olympian began to turn, raising a hand to defend himself, still a futile effort. Stone feinted a left jab, drawing the man's attention, then delivered a vicious front kick to the groin with his right foot. The former Olympian blocked part of the blow, but it still connected with devastating force, sending shockwaves of pain through his abdomen. Tears welled up in his eyes as his body betrayed him, his right hand dropping to cradle his shattered groin.

Stone wasted no time. He could have easily gone for a knockout blow, but he needed to disable the man entirely. He moved to the giant's side and executed a roundhouse kick to the man's inner thigh, targeting the tendons near the knee. The man grunted in pain, dropping lower as his legs buckled. Without hesitation, Stone circled and struck again, this time hitting the outside of the knee with a sickening snap as the ACL tore from the impact.

The giant howled, collapsing onto the rug, his body folding into itself in a fetal position. Tears streamed down his face, his massive frame shuddering as he vomited from the excruciating pain.

For a moment, the room was dead silent.

The rug guards, sensing the fall of their champion, began to move toward Stone, but the crowd erupted before they could intervene. The air filled with stomping feet and smashing champagne glasses as spectators screamed their approval. The noise was deafening, a chaotic mix of excitement and violence. Several overzealous guests even shoved each other, lost in the frenzy until security stepped in to calm the chaos.

The triumphant atmosphere was cut short by the sudden blare of trumpets. The crowd fell silent, eyes turning toward the panel of dignitaries. The elderly man, displeased, rose from his seat, casting a scornful glance at the fallen giant before walking off to the side. His departure was a signal, and security began to encircle Stone.

But then, the woman— the one who had voiced concern earlier—moved. She worked her way through the crowd with purpose, her long, athletic legs carrying her to a position closer to Stone. Her slit ballroom dress swayed with each step as she gracefully maneuvered past other spectators.

"Bravo!" she shouted, her voice clear above the lingering murmur of the crowd. She clapped, louder this time, drawing extra eyes to her.

Many picked up the chant, voices growing in strength. "Bravo!" they echoed.

The senior leader paused mid-step, turning back to survey the room. His chilly eyes fell on Stone, who stood still, bruised and battered but far from beaten. The older man grunted, exchanged words with a man besides him, then gestured to someone near the exit. Moments later, guards appeared, dragging the ex-Olympian's broken body from the rug like a defeated bull in a Spanish corrida.

Stone's gaze shifted back to the panel, committing each face to memory. There were five in total, including a woman. Her high cheekbones and cruel smile offset by a slight asymmetry in her features—likely the result of cosmetic work. She was older than she appeared, and the cold gleam in her eyes suggested a ruthlessness Stone knew all too well. The gray-bearded man in the center, however, was the one to watch. His sallow complexion betrayed poor health, but his authority was absolute. The additional three men, with their strong family resemblance, sat impassively.

Inbreeders, Stone thought darkly, a wry smile tugging at the corner of his mouth.

The panel's apparent leader gestured for the music to resume, and the crowd settled back into their seats. Fresh drinks served, and the broken glass was swept away. Stone stood on the rug, his mind already working through what came next.

He had survived this round. But the night was far from over.

CHAPTER 53

Let It Play Out

The cheers reverberated through the hall, a cacophony of voices merging into a single roar. Stone scanned the crowd, focusing on the average-height, balding man who had taken center stage. He couldn't place the man's age—thirties, maybe forties—but his round belly contrasted sharply with his muscular forearms. He was visibly out of shape compared to the others, yet his confidence was unshaken. The man jumped up, slapping high fives with one or two in the crowd before kissing a beautiful woman on the lips, eliciting once more wave of laughter and hoots.

Stone noted the panel's shift in demeanor. A few minutes ago, they had appeared tense, but now, they seemed more relaxed, even amused. The music stopped abruptly, and the announcer pranced into the center of the rug, his voice booming as he gestured toward Stone and his new adversary. The electric board flickered to life, numbers spinning as the crowd scrambled to place their bets through the apps on their phones.

Stone's arm throbbed, the pain shooting up to his shoulder. He cradled it close to his body, trying to keep the discomfort at bay. He glanced at the board. The odds had evened out. The room erupted once again in deafening cheers. His opponent, the man with the swagger and too copious bravado, laughed and mocked the crowd. His overconfidence was palpable, but Stone had seen enough. He shook his head, stepping back, aware of the men now closing in behind him. His legs and arms now free. They were aware, as was he. This wasn't a brute force fight anymore; this was something else entirely.

Silence descended on the room like a heavy shroud. The announcer pointed at Stone, gesturing for him to step forward and face his opponent. Stone shook his head more vigorously this time, refusing to play into their game.

The panel exchanged glances, the atmosphere growing tense once again. They were not pleased. The local favorite, their star fighter, was defeated by a foreigner, and now he was refusing to continue the entertainment. A man on the panel leaned into the older leader's ear, whispering something. The sheik nodded, then barked out an order in rapid Arabic. The announcer's eyes widened for a fraction of a second before he activated his microphone again.

"Ladies and gentlemen," the announcer's voice dripped with mockery, "our guest tonight does not wish to entertain us any longer." Boos erupted from the audience. Stone remained still, the jeers washing over him like white noise. The odds of him leaving this place alive had already plummeted to zero the moment he'd taken out their star. He had nothing to lose but his life.

"Or…" The announcer raised a hand, signaling for silence. "We could watch this instead."

All eyes turned to the massive screen as the electric board faded and a video feed blinked on. The timer in the upper right-hand corner ticked forward. The camera focused on a high-backed chair; a figure slumped in it. As it zoomed in, Stone felt his breath catch for a second. He showed no extra sign of emotion. The panel watched him tentatively, waiting for a reaction, disappointed by his stoic expression.

The camera slowly panned upward, revealing a pair of well-manicured feet, then legs, tied at the ankles. As the lens climbed higher, a woman's sobs became audible. Her hands bound above her head, her hair disheveled, her dress torn. A hand jerked her head up, revealing her face.

Catherine.

Stone's heart stopped for an instant, but his face betrayed nothing. The panel stirred, sensing something shift in him. The announcer smirked.

"You fight, or she dies."

Stone's mind went into overdrive. He couldn't save her from here; he knew that much. They must've caught her after she left the hotel. He should've never involved her. The guilt gnawed at him, but it wouldn't help him now. He had to focus. He had to calculate how many men he could take with him before they killed him. He wanted to get to the older leader, but the distance was too great. The guards would intercept him before he got close.

His thoughts were interrupted by a blood-curdling scream. The screen instantly regained everyone's attention. Catherine's captor pressed a knife under her chin, the blade biting into her throat. The man grinned as the camera zoomed in on his sadistic smile.

CHAPTER 54

Katana

Yoise savored the moment, standing over the American woman. He foresaw the events to come. Stone would snap, try to kill as many as he could before they brought him down. It was perfect. Stone would be out of the way, and Yoise could deal with the remaining family members at his leisure.

The announcer turned his attention back to Stone, a smug look plastered on his face. The crowd picked up on the tension, beginning to taunt Stone, but he remained unmoved. Disregarding their jeers, darkness fell on the screen, and the numbers reappeared. Bets resumed, odds shifting now to two-to-one against Stone. No one believed he had a chance—nor that the girl would survive.

The man in the center, their fighter, danced around, shadowboxing to amuse the crowd. Stone's advance was slow and methodical. The crowd surged forward as well, eager for the night's final bloodbath.

Stone rolled his shoulders, rotating his head to ease the tension building in his neck. His muscles ached, the strain from his injuries catching up to him. He approached the rug, closer to the panel. Almost at once, the guards moved to block his path. The panel laughed, enjoying the spectacle.

His opponent feigned innocence, raising his hands as if to

show he wasn't going to fight. The crowd chuckled knowingly, understanding what would follow. He walked to a nearby box that had escaped Stone's attention. Humming to himself, the man pulled out a long cloth-wrapped object.

With a dramatic flourish, he unveiled a Japanese katana. The blade gleamed under the lights, and the crowd became ecstatic. Opera music began to play once more, heightening the absurdity of the scene.

Stone's thoughts flashed back to Japan, to summers spent with his best friend Koki and his grandfather's dojo. He had trained with the best, learning the deadly art of kenjutsu. This man, Drewee, was no master. He remained an amateur, a pretender playing at being a samurai. Stone knew the moves—he could predict before they happened.

Japanese swordsmanship took decades to learn, most quit before mastering these physical abilities. Only great masters would achieve the spiritual side of wielding a weapon of such caliber.

Drewee started circling, jabbing with the sword, staying out of arm's reach. Stone didn't flinch. His attention was on Drewee's feet, not the sword. That's where the real danger would come from. Drewee raised the sword above his head, a classic Katsugu, preparing for a downward strike. The crowd cheered, expecting a quick kill.

In classic kendo, shikake waza or person started attacking strikes moves forward in a straight line. The counter if one has a sword would be to try a harai waza. You flip your opponent's sword up or down with yours. It is commonly used to make an opening and strike.

But Stone moved in, fast and fluid. Drewee hesitated, confused by the sudden aggression. He had never faced an opponent who came at him. Stone hooked Drewee's sword arm with his right forearm, spinning him downward with a precise maki waza judo throw. Drewee hit the ground hard, gasping for breath. Stone wasted no time. He picked up the sword and stabbed Drewee in the neck, watching as his life drained away in a sickening gurgle.

The crowd gasped, the cheers fading into shocked murmurs. Stone didn't pause. With the sword still dripping with blood, he charged the panel. Chaos erupted as guards scrambled to stop him.

The woman who complained about Stone's injuries walked closer to the panel area. She remained nearby, her elbows brushing against the wealthy attendees. The guards stared at the beautiful woman in the revealing designer dress, never stopping her progression. They scanned her with a wand for weapons before she entered the building and again before entering the hall. She was greater than eye candy; she was the weapon.in the crowd—Stone hadn't noticed her before—moved toward the panel as well, her elegant dress barely concealing the lethal grace in her movements. She was a weapon, not mere decoration. Stone's instincts flared to life. She possessed more depth than was visible.

As she took out a guard with ruthless efficiency, she sprang to life, striking the guard closet to her with a ridge knife hand strike to his left ear, stunning the man before she kneed him in the groin and pulled his SIG Sauer P320. She proved proficient in all major sidearms. She switched the safety and pulled the trigger point blank at the guard's head. The room descended into pandemonium. A secondary explosion came from two sets of doors around the hall. Automatic weapons shook the room in all directions. Gunfire erupted; the guards were overwhelmed by the sudden attack from two tactical teams. Stone seized the moment, using the confusion to close the distance between him and the leader.

The fight remained unfinished, but the tide had turned. And Stone had more to do.

In the commotion, the woman, weapon pointed, sprinted toward the panel, pushing her way through the crowd of screaming and falling bidders.

Stone adrenal kicked in high gear, running at the two guards in front of the panel protecting the leader. He heard gunfire and thought a different guard shot at him. He picked up the pace, running bent over. The guard on his right drew his weapon on Stone from less than half a meter away. Stone's speed was superior. He thrust the point at the man's right shoulder. He could have aimed for the simpler central target; however, he understood the blade might become lodged in the guard's stomach, or, even worse, deflect harmlessly if body armor shielded him. Stone pushed through, driving the sword in while planting himself into a front stance and executed a reverse punch with his left fist, striking the second guard in the throat.

With the sword released, Stone brushed past both falling men. The people on the panel hastily exited the hall while the remaining guards engaged the threats behind them. Darkness fell upon the grand hall as screams from the audience intensified their panicked dash for the exits amid the chaotic spray of gunfire. The woman emptied her gun on the remaining guards as the breaching team neutralized any remaining threats in the hall. Her earnings have a beacon tracker, and the team leader approached her.

"Well," in Hebrew to the woman.

"It's about time," her response as she extended her hand for his sidearm.

"The traffic is unbelievable this time of night," served as his only defense; he offered a small shrug. His blond hair remained in place, irritating her further as she left for Stone and the leader's group. Two of the breaching team and blond commando reloaded and ran after her.

The three guards surrounded the older leader while the rest of the group ran down the passage with the emergency lights kicking in to illuminate towards an exit of the building. Stone fast on their heels.

CHAPTER 55

Escape

The leader ordered the largest of his bodyguards to stay behind and finish the enemy chasing them. The aged man was not fit to outrun his pursuers without this precaution. All the guards wore earpieces for communication and serious assault rifles, none spoke a word when the order was given. The guard left behind swore to himself and looked around for the best position to lay down suppressive fire and hoped he would join his team in time to escape.

Stone stumbled into the corridor, his body starting to shut down, adrenal leaving his system. Fatigue, muscles cramping and his right arm was like dead weight. He realizes Catherine's only chance was if he could get to the old man. Stone pushed himself to move further down the hallway with infrequent light bulbs lighting the way.

Shadows every few meters allowed him to rest and refocus his vision in the darkness. It was apparent that the personal bodyguards were more tactical than the hired staff in the great hall the way they moved the leader out and covered him. Stone realized that sufficient manpower would leave one, if not two, men behind to defend.

He braced himself against the wall when he noticed a bend and the elevator sign exit. He smelled rather than saw the large shadow coming at him from the same side he was on. Stone was running out of steam; he recoiled as the butt end of a rifle came riming at his head.

The brute force smashed the gun against the cement wall, the guard grunted with the force and tried to right himself for another swing. Stone's only defense second time was to slide into the oncoming blow and encircled his legs around the man's ribcage driving his weight up and around the bigger man while Stone's forearm pressed against the guard's trachea, his grip like iron as he applied crushing pressure. The huge man squirmed, his body resisting the inevitable, but Stone held firm, clamping his forearm tighter with his opposite arm. He heard the satisfying pop of a rib snapping under the strain, and for a fleeting moment, he thought victory was near. Sweat poured from the guard's face, glistening under the dim hallway lights, his animalistic grunts growing more desperate.

Then, with a ferocious roar, the guard thrust his massive frame onto Stone, slamming him into the bitter, hard wall. The impact sent a dull thud through Stone's skull, dazing him, but he refused to loosen his hold. Sliding down the guard's back, Stone twisted, dragging the man's head with him, attempting to cut off his breath.

The guard, gasping and wide-eyed, made one final move. His hand darted behind his back.

Suddenly, a deafening blast echoed through the narrow corridor. The air seemed to freeze in place as a flash of light blinded Stone. Both men collapsed to the floor, a chaotic tangle of limbs. Stone, now on top, rolled off in a daze. His legs gave way, and he collapsed beside the guard, struggling for breath.

Tactical lights swarmed the hallway, beams bouncing off the blood-splattered wall. Footsteps thundered closer, as Stone blinked through the spots in his vision. The guard's lifeless body was before him—a gruesome exit wound where half of his forehead had been, brain matter oozing onto the floor.

The bright lights temporarily blinded Stone, his head spinning. He caught snippets of Hebrew being shouted as shadows raced by him, heading toward the elevator. A calm, controlled voice spoke near his ear, gentil yet authoritative.

"Everything's under control, R. We've got this."

He sensed hasty hands check him over before the woman moved on. Exhausted, Stone lay still, forcing his breath to slow. He tried to focus, to regulate his heart rate, but consciousness slipped from his grasp before he could steady himself.

CHAPTER 56

Necker Hospital

The Necker Hospital in Paris catered to the elite—celebrities recovering from lavish indulgences, foreign dignitaries' wives discreetly delivering their heirs, and aristocrats indulging in their latest cosmetic procedures. Its halls buzzed with the quiet confidence of Europe's finest physicians, skilled hands that mended the wealthy and the powerful. Paparazzi kept at bay across the street, their lenses waiting for a glimpse of the famous clientele. The highly compensated staff worked efficiently, accustomed to armed bodyguards standing sentinel outside private rooms. Gossip was kept to hushed tones, behind closed doors, and always in whispers.

Stone awoke to the sound of laughter—two older men, seating at the foot of his bed, their voices loud in the sterile room.

"Ah, the mishegas is finally awake!" boomed General Bondmann, his thick Israeli accent unmissable. The word meant "crazy person," and Bondmann wore it with a smirk.

WeisBerger, the heavier man seated across from him, chuckled and patted Stone's foot. "Slept well, didn't you? You're lucky your friend showed up when she did."

"Help? She saved his tuchus!" Bondmann erupted in laughter, slapping his knee.

Before Stone could gather his thoughts, a familiar voice floated in from the doorway. Soft, yet commanding.

"Are you already giving him a hard time?" Gabriella stood framed in the doorway, the corridor light casting a halo around her face. Her hair pulled back into a sleek ponytail, and the sight of her made Stone's heart pound.

The machines above his bed beeped faster. WeisBerger glanced at the monitor, then burst into another fit of laughter. "See what you've done now!" he pointed, tears of amusement rolling down his face.

"Alright, enough of you two," Gabriella waved them out, pretending to shoo them like children. "Out, before I call the nurse and have both of you vaccinated with something you've never heard of."

Still chuckling, the men shuffled out, whispering conspiracies as they left.

Gabriella crossed the room, her expression softening as she approached Stone. She checked his monitors and then gently took his pulse, though her hand lingered on his wrist a moment longer than necessary.

"You always had a knack for getting hurt," she teased, lightly patting his arm. "Rotator cuff tear and ten stitches in the forearm. You'll live."

Stone's voice came out in a rasp. "Good to know." He felt like he'd been run over by a truck. His body ached in places he didn't even realize he had.

Gabriella folded her arms, her tone turning playful but with an edge. "You know you blew our mission, right? We spent over a year tracking that group, and you came crashing in like some American cowboy."

He winced, offering a half-hearted grin. "Sorry about that."

Her gaze softened again, and she lowered her voice. "It's been so long… us. I didn't know what to expect." She glanced at the floor, the unspoken weight of their history hanging between them. He smiled gently, letting her words flow over him without interruption.

For over half an hour, Gabriella recounted the mission, her frustrations, and their tangled past, as Stone lay back, his body recovering but his mind wide awake. Eventually, the nurse appeared, insisting Gabriella leave so her patient could rest.

Gabriella argued, insisting she was also a medical professional, but Stone smiled, the tension easing from his face as the door closed behind her.

CHAPTER 57

Recovery

Stone shifted in his hospital bed; the room faint lit by the television flickering with news coverage. His body ached, bandages tight on his forearm, and his shoulder throbbed with every subtle movement. The latest headline rolled across the screen: "Foreign Special Forces clash at Louvre; French authorities struggle to regain control." The footage looped again, blurry cellphone videos of gunfire, masked men, and chaos unfolding beneath the iconic glass pyramid.

WeisBerger stood by the bed, his eyes locked on the screen, but his mind clearly elsewhere. Then spoke. "Catherine's alive. Bruised, but she fought back hard—doctors found skin under her nails. She gave as much as she got. They're running tests now to find the bastard who attacked her."

Stone's eyes narrowed as he listened, the news blared loudly in the background. His mind raced, not with the pain of his injuries, but with the events of the past few days. The knife at Catherine's throat, the bloodshed at the Louvre, and the promises left unfinished.

WeisBerger continued, a grim smile tugging at his lips. "The Israelis doubled her salary and got her out of here fast. First-class on Air France, headed back to the States. She's promised herself never to step foot in the Middle East again." He chuckled, however there was no humor in his eyes. "Can't blame her."

A moment passed before WeisBerger's voice dropped lower. "She left you a message. The man who had the knife... he let her live. Said you did him a favor when you killed the guy with the sword. Claimed you'd meet again."

Stone didn't respond, his mind already miles away, processing every implication. This was far from over. It was a debt, and debts like these never truly closed. The media frenzy outside the hospital was the least of his concerns.

News continued to flood in. Reports of the Special Forces operation at the Louvre filled every screen in the building. The French press was spinning the involvement of foreign operatives, trying to paint the chaos as a "collaborative intelligence effort." But Stone knew better. This was a botched mission, and the world was watching. The French government had been caught flat-footed, and the repercussions would echo for months, if not years.

WeisBerger grabbed the remote, flicking the TV off. "It's almost convincing, isn't it?"

Stone raised a brow. "Some got away."

The silence between them was thick, interrupted by the faint beeping of machines around Stone's bed. Gabriella came by every day to change his dressings, her touch a rare comfort amidst the chaos. His shoulder would need surgery, but the hospital staff assured him he'd heal faster than they expected. French hospitality, Stone thought wryly.

Gabriella herself pulled into the aftermath. Offered a high-profile role at the Louvre—a forensic review of stolen and forged antiquities, courtesy of a request from the President of France himself. Her skills were unmatched, and there was no one better suited for the job. Yet the layers of deception surrounding the thefts ran deep, and the task ahead of her was monumental. It would take more than just her sharp mind to unravel the truth.

Stone had spent days being debriefed by a revolving door of officials—French, Swiss, CIA, Israeli. Each session was more exhausting than the previous, the questions blending as they probed every detail of the failed mission. Even the Ambassador, who was recovering several floors above, refused to talk. Diplomatic immunity, they called it. But Stone knew better. The man was neck-deep in illegal operations: money laundering, human trafficking, antiquities smuggling. The French authorities were doing everything in their power to prosecute him, but bureaucracy was dragging its feet.

Bondmann, with his usual swagger, had dropped by earlier with a proposition. "More money. Greater perks. Mediterranean beaches. Gabriella," he added with a smirk, knowing Stone couldn't help but react to her name. The general was adept at influencing people. "We could use someone like you. No one plays the game better."

Stone wasn't buying it. "I'm not your man."

Bondmann had laughed it off. "We're all on the same team here. Just a different jersey, that's all. But you should think about it. We could get some real work done."

WeisBerger, sitting remaining silent until now, spoke. "Don't worry, Stone. No one's shipping you off anywhere. You've earned your stripes." He checked his watch. "I've got a meeting, but I'll be back tomorrow."

Stone nodded, watching WeisBerger leave the room. His body was exhausted, but his mind was still sharp, dissecting every detail of the past few days. After a half-hour of restless planning, he got up, ignoring the pain in his shoulder. He slipped into his robe and slippers, making his way to the door.

His private Israeli security detail flanked him as usual, always a step ahead and a step behind. "Just stretching my legs," Stone muttered, pushing past them. He was already used to their silent, unblinking presence. They shadowed his every move, no questions asked.

He hit the stairwell, working his way down and up again, pushing through the pain. By now, both guards had grown accustomed to his routine. He moved without hesitation, purposefully skipping his floor and heading two stories higher.

Stone reached the nurse's station and surveyed the scene. The guards stationed strategically, one at the suite corner and an extra near the elevator. It was standard, methodical, but Stone had noticed every detail. He nodded toward the elevator, gesturing upwards. His bodyguards exchanged glances but said nothing, following his lead.

Back in his room, the nurse scolded him for pushing himself too hard, but Stone's mind was elsewhere. He had gathered intel during his brief walk, information he needed. It wasn't a lot; however, it was enough for now.

Days passed in a blur of therapy and debriefings. Stone took to roaming the halls, using every spare moment to build strength and stamina. His guards grew relaxed, almost used to his constant wandering. Gabriella's nightly visits were a welcome distraction, her smile cutting through the tension in the air. She talked about her work at the Louvre, the endless bureaucracy, and the layers of deceit she was uncovering. Stone listened, his mind always half a step ahead, calculating the subsequent step.

As the week drew to a close, Gabriella asked him the question that had been hanging in the air. "So, have you thought about the General's offer?"

With eyes fixed on the darkening Paris skyline, Stone offered no immediate response. His thoughts drifted upwards, to the luxury suite two floors above. "I'm still considering my options," he muttered.

Gabriella smiled, leaning in to kiss him softly, her touch lingering longer than usual. Each understood the inherent high risk. More choices and consequences await tomorrow. And Stone would be ready regardless.

CHAPTER 58

Silent Retribution

Stone awoke just after 2 a.m., the hospital's sterile quiet wrapping him in a shroud of stillness. He slid out of bed without a sound, barefoot this time. The slippers had betrayed him before, their soft shuffle too noticeable in the silence. His nightly routine had become second nature—creeping through the hospital, mapping out security patterns, memorizing the cleaning crew's meticulous schedule. Routine was human nature, and Stone had always been adept at exploiting it.

He climbed the stairwell, reaching two floors higher. The dim lights in the hallway flickered as he stepped out, casting lingering shadows that danced along the walls. The nurse on call was slumped in her chair, her body relaxed in the false comfort of a dozing hour, the current medical resident hunkered down hours before after their last rounds. All of them unaware of his presence. The floor was still—no emergencies, no patients in critical condition. Everything was calm, just as he anticipated.

Stone paused by the elevators, glancing at the two guards posted there. They had long abandoned any semblance of diligence. The ambassador's staff had made it clear that their prying into international affairs wasn't welcome, so they no longer bothered with unnecessary rounds. Stone smirked. They were babysitting a man they likely despised—an opportunist hiding behind diplomatic immunity, linked to theft, murder, and countless other atrocities.

He entered the dimly lit doctors' lounge without waking the resident. Smocks hung in neat rows, clean gowns waiting for the next shift. Stone slipped one on over his T-shirt and sweatpants, careful to conceal the bandages on his arm. He checked himself in the mirror, adjusting his makeshift disguise, before stepping into the hallway.

The low hum of machines was the only sound that broke the silence. The automatic lights remain dimmed, casting eerie shadows along the corridor. Stone moved with purpose, passing a lone medical cart stocked with emergency supplies—syringes, sedatives, lifesaving medications. He grabbed a handful of vials and a syringe, tucking them into his pocket as he continued toward the ambassador's suite.

The room door opened without a creak. Stone slipped inside, his heart steady, his mind laser focused. The ambassador, sprawled in his oversized bed, slept under the influence of heavy sedatives. Stone had read the man's medical file. A bullet had shredded his thigh, missing vital arteries, while his abdomen had been a mess of reconstruction. The man wasn't recovering; he was withering away—unfit to face the justice he so richly deserved.

Stone went to the foot of the bed, watching the IV drip. The ambassador had insisted on its continuous flow throughout the night, a crutch to his broken body and mind. Stone's eyes narrowed. This man had profited from the misery of others— facilitating the theft of priceless art and ancient artifacts, enriching himself on the destruction of cultural heritage and the children in the camps.

Stone extracted the syringe, filling it with a fatal mix of epinephrine and norepinephrine he'd taken from the cart. His hands were steady as he injected the mixture into the IV line. He moved back and waited.

The ambassador stirred, his body twitching as the drugs began to take hold. His legs jerked, then his arms. His eyes snapped open, wide with confusion, his face contorting in a grotesque mask of panic. Stone watched as the man's respiratory system faltered, the anaphylaxis wreaking havoc on his nerves. The ambassador's mouth opened in a desperate attempt to speak, but only garbled, choking sounds escaped. His hands clawed at his throat, his eyes locking on the figure beside him—Stone, masked, cold, his green eyes unblinking.

Fear flickered in the ambassador's fading vision, his mind struggling to comprehend what was happening. Stone remained motionless, watching the man writhe. The ambassador's hand fumbled for the call button, but his muscles already betraying him. His breaths became shallow, frantic gasps, his body convulsing under the assault of the drugs.

With calculated precision, Stone drew one more syringe, this time filled with nothing but air. He injected it into the IV, sending a lethal dose of air bubbles racing through the man's veins. The ambassador's body seized, his back arching violently off the bed before collapsing, lifeless, into the sheets. His final breath was a silent scream, swallowed by the quiet of the hospital room.

Stone stood there for an additional 15 minutes; his heart rate was steady. He checked for vital signs—none. The man was gone, the weight of his crimes lifted from the world. Stone removed his gown, deposited it in the laundry bin, and discarded the vials in a biohazard box four floors below. By the time he returned to his room, slipping back into his bed, he was already fading into a deep, dreamless sleep.

A Week Later

The ambassador's sudden death made headlines for a brief moment, but no one questioned it. The official report was simple—natural causes, compounded by his extensive injuries. The French authorities had bigger fish to fry, and the media had moved on. Stone, however, knew the truth. So did Gabriella.

They spent extensive days inside the Louvre, exploring the hidden treasures buried deep beneath the museum's famed galleries. Gabriella's team, a handpicked group of Israeli anthropologists and art historians, combed through the artifacts, cataloging and identifying each one with meticulous care. Every so often, Stone would lend a hand, moving large items or helping her adjust the lighting. Gabriella had become the museum's de facto expert on stolen antiquities, her work uncovering the extent of the black-market trade that had plundered countless historical treasures.

The routine was a welcome distraction for Stone. His days were filled with coffee runs for Gabriella and her security detail, croissants in the morning, and quiet strolls through the museum after hours. But even amidst the silence, Stone's mind churned, replaying the events of the past weeks. The ambassador's death was a necessary action—retribution for the innocent lives lost. Stone, however, realized the battle was far from won.

The leader of 786 was still out there, having slipped through the French and Israeli nets during the chaos by the Seine. CCTV footage showed him parking a van at the Gare de Lyon train station, but from there, the trail went cold. The French investigators continued combing through hours of footage, hoping to catch a break. But Stone wouldn't wait. The man was a ghost, and ghosts didn't stay in one place for long.

Gabriella was appointed managing director of the Louvre by a new president, Jean-Luc Mouttalib, a former military general handpicked by the French president. The appointment brought much-needed stability to the investigation, Stone, however, knew the fight wasn't finished. Somewhere out there, the 786 leader and his accomplices were plotting their following move, and Stone would be ready when the time came.

For now, though, he had time to prepare—to heal, to plan, and to wait. The storm was far from over.

EPILOGUE

A New Path

Stone leaned back in his chair, the faint hum of the Louvre's air conditioning the lone sound in the cavernous underground room. The dim lighting cast shadows across the rows of boxes that had been hastily arranged for Gabriella's team to sift through. Artifacts, documents, and hidden treasures—pieces of history stolen, sold, and forgotten. His fingers grazed the edges of a weathered file, one that had slipped unnoticed into the bottom of a crate. Something about it caught his eye. He paused, unfolding the yellowed pages with care. And there it was—a lead, buried deep in layers of bureaucracy and dust, but unmistakable. It was the kind of find that changed everything.

The adrenaline hit him in a slow, creeping wave. This wasn't just another file. Rather a path forward, and every instinct in him screamed to follow it.

Later that evening, Stone met Gabriella at their favorite café on Île Saint-Louis. The warm lights of the Parisian streets flickered through the large windows, casting a golden hue over their table. Outside, there was the hushed flow of the Seine, its dark waters reflecting the soft glow of the streetlamps. Inside, the hum of quiet conversations filled the air, accompanied by the clinking of cutlery and the rich aroma of French cuisine.

Stone studied Gabriella for a moment. The recent events

had taken their toll on both of them, but she still carried herself with that quiet strength, her eyes sharp and attentive despite the weariness that clung to them. She glanced up from her menu, catching his gaze, and smiled.

"You look like you've got something on your mind," setting the menu down. "What is it?"

He hesitated, choosing his words carefully. This wasn't just a casual road trip he was proposing, and he realized she would sense that. "I found something today—while I was helping with those boxes in the archives. A file. I think... it could be important. Something worth chasing."

Gabriella's expression shifted, a flicker of curiosity lighting up her features. "Chasing? You're thinking of heading out again, aren't you?"

Stone nodded, leaning forward, his voice dropping as the weight of the discovery settled between them. "This is bigger than just a lead. I think this could take us to places we hadn't considered before. And I'm not talking about another museum collection. This goes deeper."

She studied him for a moment, her eyes narrowing as she processed his words. The intensity in her gaze told him she understood the gravity of what he was proposing. Stone could feel the tension rise between them, unspoken but palpable.

"And where does this lead take you?" she asked, though he could hear the answer already forming in her mind.

"Japan," Stone replied, his tone calm but filled with purpose. "I need to reach out to an old friend—someone who might have answers, or at least a direction. The kind of man who can navigate these waters better than anyone. But it's been a long time. I'm not even sure if he's still... available."

Gabriella's brow furrowed, her fingers absently tracing the edge of her glass. "And you're sure this is worth it? After everything that's happened?"

Stone's gaze never wavered. "I can't ignore it, Gabriella. Not after what we've uncovered. This could be the key to unlocking something considerable. It's not just about recovering artifacts anymore. This feels like a final piece of a puzzle we didn't even know we were building."

Silence hung between them for a moment, the sounds of the café fading into the background as they both considered the implications. Gabriella finally nodded, a quiet understanding passing between them. She trusted his instincts—she always had.

"Then let's do it," she whispered, her voice calm. "But I'm coming with you. We're in this together."

Stone felt a surge of gratitude but kept it buried beneath his stoic exterior. He gave her a small nod, appreciating her resolve. "First things first," he said, breaking the tension with a slight grin. "I need to brush up on some old skills. If I'm going to track down this lead, I need to be sharp. And for that... I need an invitation."

Gabriella raised an eyebrow, intrigued. "Invitation?"

Stone pulled out his phone, scrolling through his contacts until he landed on the name he hadn't reached out to in years. His closest friend from Japan—a man with connections and abilities that few in the world possessed. A master in more ways than one.

"I'll send him an email," Stone suggested fingers hovering

over the screen. "It's been a long time, and I'm not sure if he'll respond. But if anyone can help us find what we're looking for, it's him."

Gabriella watched him, her curiosity now mixed with cautious optimism. "And if he doesn't respond?"

Stone met her gaze, his expression unreadable. "Then we find another way."

The gravity of his words hung in the air as the night deepened. Outside, the city moved on, unaware of the quiet storm building between them. Stone recognized the road ahead would be dangerous, filled with uncertainty and shadows. But he had always thrived in the shadows—where the lines between right and wrong blurred, and the stakes were life or death.

He sent the email, a message to an old friend, a request for guidance in the search for something of far greater value than treasure. Then, with the weight of his decision pressing on his shoulders, he looked back at Gabriella.

"Whatever happens," he whispered, "we need to be ready."

Gabriella nodded. They both recognized that the journey ahead would change everything, and nothing would ever be the same.

Outside, the Seine flowed steadily, indifferent to the choices made above its waters. But inside, at a small café on Île Saint-Louis, the first steps of a new mission being laid out—one that would take Stone and Gabriella across continents, into the heart of a mystery that could alter the course of history once again.

ACKNOWLEDMENTS

I've lost track of how many years I've spent writing this novel—revising, setting it aside, then coming back to it time and again. I began writing on airplanes headed to family vacations and while waiting to pick up my kids from school. They're all grown now but just like with my other books over the years, I owe them so much for their encouragement, patience, and insight.

My love of reading began with my mother, who took me to the library and let me check out as many books as I could carry. That joy hasn't changed—we still go to the library together and leave with our arms full of stories waiting to be read.

My father shared with me his love for action movies. We watched them together on TV or at the theater, and decades later, he continued that tradition with my kids. They'd sit on his lap, share popcorn, and lose themselves in the adventure on screen. Those were some of the happiest moments for all of us. He always asked when my next book would be finished and inspired my passion for storytelling. He was the best storyteller I've ever known—always ready with a funny story at a moment's notice.

I want to thank my son Brandon for his relentless patience whenever I asked, "Could this be done?" about some bit of technology in the book. His quick reply was always, "Sure—just do this and that, and it could work." His enthusiasm and curiosity about how technology shapes our lives never cease to amaze me.

To my daughter Rachel—whose love of reading, attending author talks, and visiting book signings continually inspires me—you are the light that reminds me to say, "Why not?" whenever I have a wild idea. Your humor and perspective make life richer in every way.

I am forever grateful to my partner, Nancy, for reading and re-reading countless chapters, offering suggestions, and encouraging me by comparing my writing to other authors. Whether true or not, those words gave me the confidence to keep going. The laughter we share always brings a smile on my face when I think of our future and the adventures ahead.

And finally, thank you—the reader—for picking up this book and stepping into the world I created. If you've ever thought about writing, my advice is simple: go for it. I hope you enjoyed this story and that you'll join me again for the next adventure with Dr. Stone.